ONCE UPON
Another TIME

ALSO BY JAMES RILEY

The Once Upon Another Time series

Tall Tales

The Half Upon a Time series

Half Upon a Time

Twice Upon a Time

Once Upon the End

The Story Thieves series

Story Thieves

The Stolen Chapters

Secret Origins

Pick the Plot

Worlds Apart

The Revenge of Magic series

The Revenge of Magic

The Last Dragon

The Future King

The Timeless One

The Chosen One

ONCE UPON *Another* TIME

JAMES RILEY

ALADDIN
NEW YORK LONDON TORONTO SYDNEY NEW DELHI

ALADDIN

An imprint of Simon & Schuster Children's Publishing Division

1230 Avenue of the Americas, New York, New York 10020

First Aladdin paperback edition July 2022

Text copyright © 2022 by James Riley

Cover illustration copyright © 2022 by Vivienne To

Also available in an Aladdin hardcover edition.

All rights reserved, including the right of reproduction in whole or in part in any form.

ALADDIN and related logo are registered trademarks of Simon & Schuster, Inc.

For information about special discounts for bulk purchases, please contact Simon & Schuster Special Sales at 1-866-506-1949 or business@simonandschuster.com.

The Simon & Schuster Speakers Bureau can bring authors to your live event.

For more information or to book an event contact the Simon & Schuster Speakers Bureau at 1-866-248-3049 or visit our website at www.simonspeakers.com.

Book designed by Laura Lyn DiSiena

The text of this book was set in Adobe Garamond Pro.

Manufactured in the United States of America 0622 OFF

2 4 6 8 10 9 7 5 3 1

The Library of Congress has cataloged the hardcover edition as follows:

Names: Riley, James, 1977- author.

Title: Once upon another time / by James Riley.

Description: First Aladdin hardcover edition. | New York : Aladdin, 2022. |
Series: Once upon another time ; 1 | Audience: Ages 8 to 12. | Summary: Lena has a problem: she is a twelve-year-old giant child, but she is still only the size of a human. Rejected by the giant king, she and her enormous talking cat, Rufus, go down to the human world seeking some magic that will restore her to her rightful status. Jin is a twelve-year-old genie, not yet allowed his full powers, and at the moment tied—for two more wishes—to the Golden King, an annoying, nasty tyrant who has sent him on a quest. When these two children meet, all the kingdoms may be changed forever.

Identifiers: LCCN 2021026232 (print) | LCCN 2021026233 (ebook) |
ISBN 9781534425873 (hardcover) | ISBN 9781534425880 (paperback) |
ISBN 9781534425897 (ebook)

Subjects: LCSH: Giants—Juvenile fiction. | Jinn—Juvenile fiction. | Magic—Juvenile fiction. |
Cats—Juvenile fiction. | Fairy tales. | Quests (Expeditions)—Juvenile fiction. | Adventure stories. |
CYAC: Giants—Fiction. | Genies—Fiction. | Magic—Fiction. | Cats—Fiction. | Fairy tales. |
Adventure and adventurers—Fiction. | LCGFT: Fairy tales. | Action and adventure fiction.

Classification: LCC PZ7.1.R55 On 2022 (print) | LCC PZ7.1.R55 (ebook) | DDC [Fic]—dc23

LC record available at https://lccn.loc.gov/2021026232

LC ebook record available at https://lccn.loc.gov/2021026233

To anyone living with their head in the clouds.

Watch out for giants up there!

ONCE UPON
Another TIME

CHAPTER 1

Lena held her breath as she slipped beneath a door that was easily one hundred feet tall and caught sight of the giant, snoring loudly in the kitchen as a fire flickered in the dim light. The wooden chair he lounged in looked like it could barely hold his weight, and it creaked with every tiny movement.

Hopefully, that creaking would cover any sounds she made, since she knew that if the giant woke up before she could find her treasure, this was all over. Fortunately, even at five and a half feet tall, taller than the average human twelve-year-old, she still measured barely a tenth of the giant's height, so her footsteps were basically silent.

Unfortunately, the item she was after was currently sitting in the giant's tunic pocket. And that was going to present some problems.

Something large and fuzzy pushed into her from behind, and she absently reached back to scratch her cat, Rufus, beneath his floppy feathered hat. Rufus himself was about the size of a horse, a few inches taller than Lena when sitting on his haunches, but he moved more quietly than she did even with his boots on, assuming he wanted to.

To Lena's disappointment, he didn't seem to want to.

"We are in the food room, but do not eat?" the long-haired tabby cat asked, too loudly for Lena's comfort. "This makes no sense to Rufus."

"Shh, little man," she said, wondering if she should remove his magical hat for now, since that was what gave him the ability to speak in her language. But if she did, he wouldn't understand her, either, and that could get them in trouble. "I'll get you a treat later, okay? Right now, we need to get up there." She pointed at the giant's chest, slowly rising and falling with every snore.

Rufus's whiskers twitched. "*Two* treats?"

She smiled in spite of the tension. "Sure, two treats. But now we are going to be quiet, okay? No waking him up."

Rufus blinked and crept forward at her side, seeming to get the message. She had toyed with the idea of leaving him behind, but in the event she needed to make a quick escape, the Seven League Boots on her cat's feet would make all the difference. Not that she knew exactly how far a league was, but the boots let their wearer leap great distances in seconds, and that was good enough for her.

Plus, alongside his floppy translating hat, they just made Rufus look so fancy.

The wooden floor of the giant's house had enough cracks in it to make Lena have to carefully pick her way over to the kitchen chair, and she didn't have any time to waste. Even if the giant didn't wake up, his wife might be home soon, and then Lena would be caught instantly. And slowly making her way across the kitchen floor was taking far too long.

"Can you carry me up to the kitchen table, little man?" she whispered to Rufus, and climbed up on his back.

He twitched his whiskers in response, then took off at a silent run, even with his boots. But instead of going toward the table as requested, he ran for a broom leaning against the nearby wall.

"No, over here!" Lena whispered in his ear, leaning forward as she pointed back toward the table. But Rufus didn't seem to hear and made a great leap straight at the broom. He hit it hard and kicked off, sending them flying in the direction of the table, though still too low to reach it. . . .

Instead, they landed hard on one of the kitchen chairs, only long enough for Rufus to catch his balance and take off again, leaping back and forth between the backs of two chairs to take them higher and higher.

Finally, they reached the top of the kitchen table, and Rufus skidded to a stop, almost throwing Lena straight over his head. She managed to hold on, then slowly dismounted, scratching her good boy behind his ears for doing so well. Okay, sure, Rufus wasn't the most graceful cat ever—she'd seen him fall off perfectly level fences twice as wide as he was—but he always tried his best, and that was all she could ever ask.

He purred as he looked over at her, clearly proud of himself. "*Three* treats?" he said, and Lena quickly looked up at the giant to see if he'd heard, but another snore told her they were still safe. She shushed her cat again but nodded, smiling a bit. He'd earned them, after all.

He purred again as he followed her over toward the giant's arm that rested on the table. Rufus had landed them relatively close to it, which was good, because she didn't know how much longer they had before the giant's wife returned. Lena tried to move as quickly as possible while still staying silent and finally reached his elbow.

The giant's tunic was loose enough for her to climb, so she grabbed a handful of fabric and easily pulled herself up to stand on top of his forearm. Rufus prepared himself for a leap to reach the same level, but she quickly shook her head, worrying that that much weight landing on the giant would awaken him. She put up her hands for Rufus to stop, and he did, looking up at her in confusion.

Confusion was basically Rufus's primary trait, with curiosity a close second, with the latter being the reason he was so much larger than other cats. If he hadn't leapt into the cauldron the Last Knight had meant for Lena . . .

The giant snorted loudly, disturbing his sleep for a moment, and turned his body enough to carry his arm out away from the table. Lena grabbed ahold of the tunic and held on tightly as the table beneath her disappeared, leaving her several dozen feet off the floor. If the giant woke up now, that would be it.

But his snoring returned to normal, and Lena let out a sigh of relief . . . at least until she heard footsteps outside.

The giant's wife. It had to be.

And that meant Lena was out of time.

She took a deep breath, then ran straight up the giant's arm, passing the elbow, then leaping toward his chest. He'd moved his arm closer to his body, so the jump wasn't difficult, but she still landed harder than she'd have liked, and the giant mumbled something in his sleep.

It was too late to worry about that now, though, so she forced herself to climb up toward his pocket, hand over hand, moving as quickly as she could. The footsteps outside drew closer, and she wondered if she'd make it to the treasure before the giant's wife reached the kitchen door. If she could just grab the item, she'd be home free, but that was still a big "if."

"Roral?" said a voice from outside. "Don't tell me you're sleeping again."

The giant below Lena immediately sat up, almost tossing her off his tunic. "Of course not!" he shouted back. "I was just . . . cleaning the kitchen!"

Clinging to the giant's shirt, Lena knew she had at most mere seconds before he noticed her. With one last burst of strength, Lena threw herself toward the pocket, snagging it with one hand, then falling neatly inside right as the front door opened and the giant's wife appeared.

"That was the best you could do, 'cleaning the kitchen'?"

she asked. "You have to make your lies more believable."

The giant laughed, shaking Lena around in his pocket, but she didn't let it stop her, not with her prize so close. Because right next to her inside the pocket was the treasure she'd come for.

She slowly reached for the enormous folded paper and pulled it open just enough to read from it.

"And where is . . . ," the giant's wife started to ask, only to stop as a loud "aha!" sounded from the giant's pocket. She looked at her husband. "I'm sorry, did you say something?"

Two enormous fingers pinched the outside of the pocket and pulled it open just enough for the creature's giant eyes to peer down inside. "Oh come *on*," the giant said, shaking his head. "Are you kidding me with this?"

Lena held up the paper triumphantly in her hands, waving it at the giant. "Nice *try*, Dad!" she shouted. "But I found the invitation, and my name's on it. I *knew* I was invited to the Ritual of the Spark this year!"

CHAPTER 2

"Once upon a time, there was a great king," said the man draped in golden robes, his arms out dramatically as he stood before a gleaming yellow throne. "No, no, not me, but that's nice of you to say."

No one *had* said, but the assembled nobles all laughed politely up and down the enormous throne room, golden statues lining it on both sides. A brown-haired, ordinary-looking boy stood in the shadows at the side of the room, rolling his eyes as he wondered how long this was going to take. Jin hated being here, and not just because of how tacky the room was, with everything in it made entirely of gold.

The nobles themselves provided the only contrast, forbidden as they were from wearing the king's color, so most were wearing silken fabrics in silver tones or other rich colors, though none wore copper or bronze, as that might be too close and offend the king.

The Golden King smiled benevolently down on his subjects. "No, this king had three sons, each one more handsome and clever than the last, which of course means the youngest was the clear winner."

He gestured at the three golden statues lined up behind the throne, and from a distance, Jin could tell that the statues didn't look too thrilled. One was older, a middle-aged man, while the other two looked to be in their early twenties. But all had terrified expressions on their faces, and the two younger ones both had their arms up as if to defend themselves.

"Wanting to ensure that only the wisest of his children would lead, the king declared that whichever of his sons brought him an item of *true power* would be his rightful heir." He paused. "Now, we all know from stories that the youngest son will outwit the others. That's just how these things work."

"So true, Your Majesty!" someone shouted out, and the king pointed at him, nodding.

"Indeed," the Golden King said. "But stay with me here.

So off these three princes went, searching the realm for items of true power, and years passed before they all returned. Finally, the three princes appeared before their aged father and presented their findings."

Jin sighed audibly. The king liked to make up holidays and anniversaries to celebrate himself, and today's Celebration of the Golden King's Family Day was among the most boring yet. Jin opened his mouth to yawn widely, only to feel his lips close in mid-yawn. Annoyed, he threw a look at the Golden King, who had just closed the fingers on his right hand, silencing Jin.

Ugh. Jin muttered some choice responses to himself, then nodded almost imperceptibly, and the magic keeping his lips closed disappeared. The Golden King flashed him a tiny smile, then went back to his speech.

This was all so degrading. Was this honestly why he was here, to let humans humiliate him like this? Was that really what the elders wanted?

And why humans? Jin squinted at the Golden King, looking down through the surface level to the light that all of his kind could see, the light of magic. It shone from any enchanted object or cast spell, but living creatures had their own kind of magic as well, and it tended to reveal their true nature, if you looked closely enough.

With the Golden King, if there was any light, it was too faint to see, blocked as it was by shadows black as night. Moving his gaze around the hall, Jin found that the rest of the humans all had at least a spark of color inside them, all but the king.

Great. Why had the worst human alive been the one to gain control over him?

"The oldest son, he brought back a darkness from a distant land," the king continued, smiling. "'Father,' he said, 'this shadow magic can create fear wherever it goes, and there's nothing that rules better than fear.'"

Someone clapped in the crowd, but the king threw them a look, and they went silent.

"'Perhaps,' said his father, 'but let us see what your brothers brought.' And then it was the turn of the middle brother, who showed off a ring, one containing a stone finer than any in the land."

Though the king didn't show the ring, Jin knew it was on his right finger, covered by a nonmagical glove. Jin could feel its power; it was what gave the Golden King control over him, after all.

11

"'This ring contains ultimate magical power,' the middle brother said. 'And that is *true* strength, the ability to force others to bow before you.'"

The assembled crowd cheered in response, and Jin clapped along loudly, wondering if the king would allow sarcastic applause. Apparently not, as Jin's hands stuck together on the second clap.

He'd only been doing this whole serving-humans-to-learn-humility thing for just over a decade now, and it was already such a massive pain in his nonexistent behind. It would have been slightly better if Jin could have served just that middle brother, at least, the one who'd actually found Jin's ring in some buried cave in a far-off land. But Jin had only granted one of that prince's wishes before the ring was—

"And finally, the youngest and most clever brother presented what we all know is the greatest power of all," the Golden King said, raising his golden glove and clenching it into a fist. "For he had found wealth, the one thing that will motivate every human being. With the gold this youngest son could make from his newfound magical glove, he could rule the entire world!"

The group of assembled nobles burst into applause, and for once, Jin wasn't sure they were faking it for the king's approval.

"Of course the youngest son was declared the winner!" the Golden King said, holding up both his hands now. "Gold *is* the only true power, so the king declared this prince the rightful heir, as is the way of these stories, and granted him both his brothers' findings as a gift."

Jin threw a look at the princes' statues behind the throne again. The looks on their faces didn't look like they'd handed over *anything* voluntarily.

"And that was how I was *meant* to become ruler of these kingdoms!" the king shouted excitedly, then paused for effect and sighed, shaking his head sadly. "And I would have too, if the people hadn't decided out of the blue to no longer abide by the right of royalty to lead, and instead *choose* their own rulers."

The crowd began to boo, and Jin joined in, only to have his mouth shut once more, as the king seemed to realize where Jin's boos were directed. If nothing else, the Golden King was pretty insightful that way, Jin had to admit.

"Still, after the fairy queen's puppet messed everything up, the people did the proper thing, and chose *me* to lead you, as was always intended," the king continued, nodding magnanimously at his assembled subjects. "And yet, there are still those who object to my rule, like the Last Knight and his horrible rebels—"

Just as the words left his mouth, a blinding light appeared in the middle of the throne room.

The crowd began screaming, and this time, Jin half wanted to join in, considering the pain in his eyes. *I shouldn't even have felt that!* he wanted to yell, but that would just get him in more trouble with the Golden King.

"Oh, hello!" said a voice from the middle of the light as it slowly dimmed, revealing a man in a glowing suit of silver armor, his helmet's visor down, concealing his face. "I thought I heard my name. Is this the castle of the Golden King?" He looked around a bit as the nobles backed away in fright. "You know, gold's really not a sturdy building material. Too soft. I'd have recommended stone."

"You!" the Golden King shouted. "The Last Knight!"

The man in the silver armor bowed low. "Nice to be recognized, even by His Highness the Ridiculous," the knight said, then stood back up. "Now, if you don't mind, I'm here for the twins. Please bring them out to me, or I might get angry."

Jin's magically created heart began to race, and he stepped forward in excitement. Finally, something interesting! He had no idea who these twins were, but the king complained about the Last Knight *constantly*. And if the rebel was here, in the throne room, this would be the perfect time to capture him.

And if the king needed to capture someone, what better way than to make a wish? Jin rubbed his hands together in anticipation. There were just two wishes left, and then he'd be *free* of this horrible king.

All in all, this whole genie thing was just such a *giant* pain.

CHAPTER 3

*O*w!" the giant yelled in pain as Lena punched him in the thumb.

"You guys told me I wasn't invited!" she yelled, giving her father a stern look as she punched his index finger now, while he tried to fish her out of his pocket. "But my name's right there on the invitation!"

"Seriously, that hurt!" the giant said, looking to his wife for sympathy, but she just rolled her eyes.

"Oh stop it, Roral," the woman said, shaking her head, then reached in and picked Lena up out of the pocket and placed her on the kitchen table. "And *you*. What have I told you about hitting your poor father?"

Lena snorted. "That's how *true* giants handle people who don't tell the truth. You know what the king says: 'Giants fight to show their might!'" She threw a few punches in the air while her father backed his chair away in fear. "And you *promised* I could go to the ritual when I was invited. Why would you tell me I wasn't?"

"Oh, I'm sorry, I didn't realize we were revealing your secret to the whole village now," her mother replied, bending down to glare at Lena while raising an eyebrow.

Lena sighed. "We should! I'm just as much a giant as the rest of them."

"Yes, you are," her mother said, giving her a slight smile. "You're also five feet tall."

"Five and a *half*," Lena said. "Which you can basically round up to six feet."

"So a *tenth* the size of the other giants," her mother said, furrowing her brow, which told Lena she was about to get lectured again. "Lena, you *know* how they feel about humans—"

"I'm a *giant*!" Lena shouted, stamping her foot and shaking the entire table below her. "Not a human!"

"And yet, if they see someone your size, that's exactly what they'll assume you are," her mother continued.

"She could wear the Growth Ring, of course," her father pointed out, then slumped down even farther in his chair after a dirty look from her mom.

"Yes, see?" Lena shouted, pointing at her dad. "The Growth Ring! No one will even know. We've done it before! I'll look exactly like every other giant."

"She's certainly got the strength of one," her father said, holding his fingers tenderly. Both his wife and daughter raised an eyebrow at the giant. "It hurts, okay? She's tougher than she looks!"

Lena rolled her eyes. "*You've* been the one teaching me the traditional way to fight like a giant for the last twelve years, Dad! Now that I'm landing hits, you suddenly can't take it?" she said, and swiped out at him again. This time he kicked back to avoid her hit only to tip the chair over, sending him crashing into the firewood behind him.

"You're being so dramatic," her mother told her dad, sighing.

"Let her hit *you* next time, and see how dramatic I'm being," her father said, picking himself up off the floor.

"So this means I can go, then? If I wear my Growth Ring?" Lena said hopefully, looking up at her parents. She'd spent far too many years just watching them go off to the Ritual of the Spark, where giants came together from across the clouds to the castle of the king of giants. And now that she was finally old enough to go at age twelve, she was beyond ready to be counted as a member of the village, along with the other giant children her age. "This would be a good way to make friends with other giant kids, you know!"

A loud, indignant meow came a moment before something huge and furry slammed against her as Rufus rubbed his head against hers. "Lena wants friends? Rufus is Lena's friend."

She laughed and reached up to scratch him behind his enormous ears. "You'll always be my *best* friend, little man," she said as he purred loudly. "But you want to come to the castle too, don't you?"

Rufus stared at her for a moment. "*This* isn't the castle?"

"No cats!" her father yelled, cleaning up the firewood. "There's no way you're bringing that thing to the ritual. We'll have enough trouble keeping *you* . . ."

He trailed off, but Lena knew what he'd been about to say, and she felt a pang in her chest. *Keeping you a secret*, he was going to say. Hiding her height, how she looked like a human, in spite of being born to two giants.

Hiding how unlike a true giant she was, how embarrassing she must be to her two giant parents.

"Roral!" her mom shouted, and her dad's face turned red. "We're not keeping you a secret, Lena. You know that they just wouldn't understand. You look so human, and after what happened to the former king all those years ago, they're . . . not the most forgiving."

Lena nodded, her brown hair falling over her face, only for Rufus to knock it back out of the way with another headbutt. "I *know* that, but—"

Her mother gave her father a long look, and after a pause, he seemed to recognize it was his turn to make excuses. "It's not about hiding you, Lena," he said. "We just don't know how they'd react. Only the king knows about your size, and he's never been the most open-minded of giants. Even the Growth Ring isn't a permanent fix—"

"She doesn't *need* a fix," her mom corrected him before turning to face Lena. "You're the exact size you're meant to be. It's the others who have it all wrong." She looked away and was silent for a few moments before continuing. "Still, you were invited, and maybe it'd cause more curiosity if you didn't come. . . ."

Lena's eyes opened wide. "Wait. So I really *can* go? That's what you're saying?" As much as she hated having to disguise who she was with the Growth Ring, the idea that she could actually go to the ritual for the first time, the ritual that only giants could attend, made her forget everything else.

Her mom smiled slightly. "*Only* with the Growth Ring. Oh, and if you *are* bringing Rufus, you'll need to hide him."

"I will! I've got the collar that shrinks him down to my size!" Lena shouted, patting the infinitely large pouch on her belt. "*Thank you, Mom!*"

Her mother reached down to hug her gently with two fingers, and Lena wrapped her arms around one of them, squeezing as tightly as she could. "Ow, hey!" her mom yelled. "That *does* hurt!"

"*See?*" her father shouted. "No one believes me until they see for themselves. She's definitely a giant!"

"Of course I'm a giant!" Lena said, grinning widely. "I'm just a compact one. I'm so excited!" She turned and leapt on Rufus's back, not wanting to waste the time running back to her room in the tiny dollhouse her parents had made for her years ago, not when Rufus could get her there so much faster.

"There are going to be *strict rules*, you know!" her mother yelled after her, but Lena didn't care. She knew there'd be all kinds of things she couldn't do or say, but that was fine. The most important thing was she was actually going to the ritual, the one that every other giant child went through at her age to become an official part of the village and receive their true last name, their epithet, like her father, Roral the Unburdened, or her mom, Cedra the Terrifying.

Lena couldn't even imagine what name the Sparktender would give her, but she knew it'd be a name only a *true* giant could live up to.

Lena would touch the Spark, just like the other giants, and get her name, just like the others. And then, *finally*, everyone would know who she really was: a true giant, just like they were.

"*Look* at this," she heard her father say from the other room, his voice booming. "I think I'm bruising!"

CHAPTER 4

"Y*OU?*" the Golden King shouted at the Last Knight, his mouth dropping open. "Guards, take him!"

Jin groaned. Guards? What a waste! Why didn't the king ask *him* instead? If he'd wished for it, Jin could have taken this knight down in a matter of moments, and the king would only have one wish left.

But *no*, the Golden King had to hoard his wishes like some greedy sort of . . . well, person who'd turn his entire castle gold.

The castle guards rushed toward the knight, their swords drawn, but the knight disappeared, reappearing just behind the king, with his oddly translucent sword held out against the king's throat, a weird white glow coming from the weapon.

"I wouldn't do that if I were you," the knight said, nodding

23

at the guards as the king shrieked in panic. "Now, I think I asked you about the twins. Would they be around, or . . . ?"

Jin blinked, wondering how the man could possibly have moved so fast. He squinted at the knight, driving down beneath the surface to examine the magical light inside, but weirdly, there was nothing there, not even the black shadows of the king.

Jin frowned. Something odd was happening here, and not just the knight's teleporting.

"Don't hurt me!" the king shouted, trembling as the knight held him. "Please, you can have anything you want! Is it gold? I can make you enough gold to last a lifetime!"

The knight released the Golden King with a disgusted snort. "You really are just a worm, aren't you?" he said. "But no, I don't care about gold. Give me the twins, and return the other rebels to me, and I'll allow you to live, though apparently without any dignity."

As the guards surrounded the king once more, he sneered at the knight. "*You* have no dignity, *you*! And now that we have you, I think it's time for you to join your friends in my statue collection."

He nodded at the side of the throne room, where golden

statues lined the wall opposite Jin. He looked over curiously, having never really examined the statues before, and realized for the first time how many of them looked just as surprised and terrified as the king's father and brothers behind the throne.

The king *was* consistent, at least.

"You shouldn't keep them out in the open like this," the knight said, also looking at the statues, though his lighthearted words were offset by the dark tone in his voice. "It's like you're daring me to steal them, and turn my friends back."

"If only you had the power to do so," the king sneered. "Get him, you fools! What do I pay you for?"

This time the knight didn't bother moving as the guards advanced and instead opened his arms wide. The closest guard reached out to capture the knight . . .

Only for his hand to pass right through the rebel.

"Oh, I'm sorry. Did I forget to mention I'm not actually here?" the knight asked, shaking his head. "So forgetful of me. Does sort of make you wonder which of your nobles helped me in."

The king, his face contorted with rage, slowly turned toward the cowering nobles before him. "One of *you* helped the rebels?" he whispered, his eyes widening.

The nobles all began talking at once, a few even dropping to their knees to swear oaths that they'd done no such thing, but the king gestured, and half the guards surrounded the nobles, pushing them out of the throne room. When they were gone, the king turned back to the knight, his face red with rage. "You've embarrassed me for the last time, you little *wretch*. I will send *all* my Faceless to find you, and there will be *nowhere* you can hide, not even in the Cursed City!"

The knight laughed. "You think you can find the Cursed City after all this time? Good luck with *that*." He turned away from the king, looking all around the room, and then he seemed to notice Jin for the first time. "And what have we here? A boy with smoke for legs?"

Jin gasped and looked down at his bottom half, realizing he'd forgotten about the magic that made him look human. "Oh, sorry!" he shouted at the knight and the Golden King. "Trick of the light. That's just, uh, smoke from the torches." He quickly solidified himself to look fully human again, wincing as he knew he'd be paying for that once the knight was gone.

The king's face looked even *more* angry at this, which Jin wouldn't have thought was possible. "Enough of this nonsense. The twins are *mine*," he hissed, leaning toward the knight.

"And you shall *never* have them. I've got an entire castle full of Faceless to guard them. But you *will* see them soon enough, once I've taken enough magic to build their power."

"So they *are* here?" the knight said, nodding. "Perfect. I figured you'd never keep them anywhere else, but I didn't want to do a whole elaborate break-in and find you'd smartened up. That's good to know, and really, all I needed, so I'll be on my way. But you're right that they'll be seeing me soon, as I'll be back when you least expect it." He began to disappear, waving goodbye at Jin.

"You're not going anywhere, you pathetic cretin!" the king roared, now much braver without the knight actually in the room. The Golden King leapt forward again with his golden glove, but the knight was gone before the king reached him, leaving the king to stumble awkwardly, almost tripping on his long golden robes.

Jin swallowed hard, wishing he hadn't just seen that. Without a word, the Golden King stood up, straightened his robes, then turned and grabbed Jin's arm as he passed, pulling him into the quiet of the adjoining hallway and then to the king's waiting room. Off in the distance, Jin could hear the nobles yelling as the guards locked them away in rooms, which probably meant that there were going to be a number of new statues in the throne room soon.

But unfortunately, Jin knew the king would be dealing with *him* first.

The Golden King's private rooms were, if anything, even more gaudy, as everything within was made of gold, from the walls to the furniture to the floor. Again, pretty tacky in Jin's mind, and not at all comfortable, either, so a lose-lose all around.

"Well, that was a surprise, Your Majesty!" Jin said as the Golden King closed the door quickly behind them. "Honestly, I think you could have taken him, if he'd really been there." He looked up at the Golden King innocently. "Or if you'd like, you could always use a wish, and—"

Any attempt by the Golden King to appear calm disappeared the moment the door closed, and he stared at Jin for a moment, his fists clenched. "My nobles betray me. The Last Knight mocks me. And now *you* have revealed one of my most powerful weapons to the enemy!"

Ah. Right. "Oh, I'm sure he didn't know what I am. There can't be *that* many genies in this world, since as far as I know, I'm the only one young enough to have to serve humans. Still, if you want to make a wish, I'm sure I could—"

The Golden King sneered, then squeezed two fingers together in response, cutting off Jin's air. Jin's eyes widened, and he put his hands to his throat, but he knew it was useless. The king had absolute control over him, up to and including making him want to breathe in the first place, something genies didn't need to do naturally. Forcing him to draw in breath, then keeping the air from reaching his lungs was just the kind of cruelty the king enjoyed.

Not that Jin could suffocate, even when in a human form, since if he fell unconscious, he'd just revert back to his gaseous, spirit state. But not breathing definitely wasn't comfortable in the meantime, and the king could make him *feel* like he might die, even if that was impossible.

"You seem to forget which of us is in control," the Golden King said quietly. "Now, are you done with your jokes? I would think a little *respect* might be in order, considering."

Jin gritted his teeth, then nodded, hating having to do it.

The king kept his fingers pressed together for another moment, only to abruptly release them. Air came flooding back into Jin's lungs, and he gasped, then took a deep breath, just enjoying the feeling, not caring if it was real or not.

The king looked down at the lower half of Jin's body. "If not

29

for the Last Knight's attack, the court might have noticed your legs were missing. Do that again, and I'll punish you for *real*."

Jin nodded again and glanced down himself to make sure the legs hadn't gone anywhere. The king insisted on keeping him around, just in case of danger, instead of letting Jin relax inside the ring, like his brother had. But that meant Jin had to disguise himself as human to hide his natural form, which was basically an intangible spirit that looked like a cloud of smoke.

Originally, Jin had chosen what he thought was a fairly handsome form, giving himself all kinds of muscles and appealing features, but the king had immediately shut that down and forced him to instead look completely forgettable, which did work, in that most humans in the castle barely even noticed Jin was there. His dark brown pants, gray shirt, and thin gray hooded cape helped with that, though Jin was just glad not to have to wear gold.

"The Last Knight has gone too far this time," the king said, pacing around as Jin finished looking himself over. "Up until now, he's just been an annoyance, interfering too often as I dealt with the magical threats to my people. But now he means to take the twins back? I will *not* allow it!"

Jin opened his mouth to ask who the twins were but decided

this wasn't the best time for questions and shut his mouth instead. Besides, the king sounded like he was about to do just what Jin was hoping he would do, so the last thing he wanted to do was distract the man.

"For my second wish, genie," the king said, turning back to glare at Jin, "I want you to capture the Last Knight from the Cursed City and bring him here, to me, *in chains*."

And *there* it was. Finally, the second wish. Just one more and he'd be free!

Jin tried to hide his excitement as he bowed low. "It shall be done, Your Majesty."

And it would be too, no matter what it took.

All Jin had to do was figure out . . . well, *how* to do it, considering how little magic he had.

CHAPTER 5

Lena happily looked herself over in the giant-sized hand mirror her mother had given her, taking up one entire wall of the dollhouse bedroom. She'd so rarely had clothes she liked, since everything her parents had provided had come from dolls.

Of course, once she'd discovered the human city on the ground below the clouds, that had all changed, but she couldn't let her parents know *that*.

While the other giants would be getting dressed up for the ritual, Lena knew that she couldn't wear anything too fancy, not without her mother wondering where she'd gotten the clothing from. But she wasn't going to wear some ill-fitting doll clothing either. So she compromised by wearing one of the more giant-looking human-made outfits she'd discovered, satisfied that at least it fit. And the magic of the Growth Ring would ensure it grew along with her, so that was helpful too.

As she checked to make sure she'd belted her tunic correctly, the mirror began to mist over, and Lena frowned. Not *this* again. That was the trouble with trying to use magic mirrors to dress yourself.

"You will meet the love of your life very soon!" the mirror said in a spooky voice.

Lena rolled her eyes. "Oh yeah?" she said, glancing over at Rufus behind her. "If they're not better than my cat, I don't care."

The mirror snorted. "Hey, no one's making any claims about them being better than anyone. I'm just making prophecies here."

"Well, don't," Lena told it. "I'm trying to get ready! And how many times do I have to tell you? I don't want to hear about any love stuff!"

"Oh come on, you never let me do anything fun," the mirror said, and a face began to appear inside the glass, a boy's face with brown hair. Lena groaned and immediately looked away, not wanting to see anything more.

This wasn't the first time the mirror had tried to show her

this 'true love' person. But Lena just couldn't bring herself to care.

"All right, stop it," Lena said, trying to sound firm. "Don't just go showing me some guy when I said I wasn't interested. I'm busy!"

"He's not *some guy*," the mirror complained. "He's the one you'll spend the rest of your life with, happily ever after!"

"Ever after what?" she asked. "What does that even mean?"

"Not really sure, honestly," the mirror admitted. "It's just part of the prophecy. Ever is like 'forever,' I imagine, so maybe you'll love him after forever?"

"Sure, I'll agree to that," Lena said, tightening her belt and turning to leave. "I'll love him after forever is over. Deal."

"Oooh, looks like he's a bad boy and will be on the other side of— Hey, wait!" the mirror shouted, but she'd already walked out, Rufus right behind her.

Even if Lena hadn't had to hurry, the mirror's ridiculous prophecies were the last thing she needed to worry about. It was always trying to predict her future, one way or another, and while it was usually right—including the time she'd discovered the mountain poking through the clouds just a few miles outside town and ended up falling down it to find the human city below—it didn't exactly help to know that ahead of time.

Inevitably, whether she wanted them to or not, the prophecies came true. So why bother with them?

And she had enough on her mind at the moment. She was going to the *ritual* and would finally be an official part of the village! Would that be the time to remove the Growth Ring and show them all her true self? A shiver of fear went down her spine at the thought of all the other giants staring down at her in surprise.

Okay, maybe not just yet. But soon. And they'd have to accept her if she had her epithet. As long as it wasn't Lena the Short or Lena the Tiny—

Wait. That wouldn't be her name, would it? She could see it now, the Sparktender seeing through to her true self and declaring her Lena the Small.

Rufus slammed into her from behind, and she realized she'd stopped in place while worrying about what was to come. What was she doing? She couldn't let her fear get her down, not today of all days!

Stepping outside her dollhouse, she moved just enough

to give herself plenty of room to grow, then pulled out the Growth Ring from her pouch. Rufus sniffed at it, recognizing what it was instantly.

"Lena grows big?" Rufus said, nuzzling her with his fuzzy face. "I come with Lena?"

She beamed and turned to scratch her cat behind the ears, knowing he hated being left at home alone. "Of course you're coming," she said. "I'm going to put your collar on to make you small, okay? That way I can hide you."

He purred, his eyes closed as she scratched. "The collar is bad. But I come, so I wear collar. I'm good boy."

She almost lost it when he called himself a good boy, but she pulled his collar from her pouch. The collar was another magical relic her parents had traded for, just for Rufus. She slid it over his head, then tightened it gently around his neck, making sure it wasn't too loose or too constricting. Then she closed the clasp, and immediately Rufus shrank down to the size of an earthbound cat, just like the humans kept as pets . . . and the same size as he was when Lena had first met him.

She shrieked in joy as she always did and picked him up, cuddling him closer. "I love when you're this size!" she shouted, and he purred loudly even as he pushed away from her, not liking to be so constrained.

"Lena let me go now," he said, his tail whapping her stomach as he twitched it with annoyance. "Lena get big, and not forget me?"

"I'd never," she said, hugging him one more time.

"Lena!" her father yelled from the kitchen. "Are you almost ready?"

"Just getting big, Dad!" she shouted back, and put Rufus up on her shoulder, then readied herself to put the Growth Ring on. Part of her felt so wrong doing this, hiding her true size, her true *self* from the other giants. But it wouldn't be for much longer! As soon as everyone knew, then she'd never have to wear the horrible thing ever again.

She took a deep breath, then slipped the ring on her finger and shot into the air too fast to even comprehend as she grew fifty feet instantly.

The whole room spun around her as it always did after such a huge shift in height, and she almost fell over before reaching out to steady herself on the wall.

"Lena is okay?" Rufus said from her shoulder, almost too

small to hear. At this size, he was basically the size of a small coin to her; not wanting him to get lost, she reached out and gently stuck him behind her ear, where he could see everything, and better yet, she could hear him, just in case she needed his support.

"Are you comfortable there?" she asked.

"I am so tall!" Rufus said, purring again, and she laughed, wanting to pet him, but worrying she might hurt him.

"You're almost always taller than me," she told him with a grin, then left to go meet her parents.

As she stepped into the kitchen, her mother froze. "Where did you get that new outfit?"

Great. Her mom was way too observant. "Oh, you know, just picked it up somewhere."

Her father looked over, frowning. "*Is* it new? I swear all her clothes look the same."

Her mother rolled her eyes, then moved in closer to Lena. "*Where* did you get that?" she repeated, whispering this time.

"I, ah, traded for it," Lena said, not able to look her mother in the eye. It wasn't a lie at all, but she hoped her mother would think she meant with another giant.

"We're going to be laaaate," her dad said, nodding up at the sun giant who'd just passed by them, waving at their village like he always did as he carried the giant flaming orb across the sky. "If we don't get there soon, we'll get bad seats."

"Coming!" Lena said, and pushed past her suspicious mother.

"You and I are going to have a *long* talk when we get home," her mother whispered as her father waved them on from outside their cottage, which looked far smaller at the moment than it usually did to Lena.

"Sounds good," Lena said, cringing. But now wasn't the time to worry about future lectures. Instead, she focused on what was to come, and what amazing name she might get.

Lena . . . the Brave? Lena the Strong?

Lena the Perpetually Grounded was probably the most likely one, but even that she'd take, if it meant finally getting to be a part of the giant village and not having to hide in her own house.

"Everyone ready?" her father asked, completely oblivious to Lena's nervousness and her mother's suspicions. "Great! This is going to be *fun*."

CHAPTER 6

From what Jin could tell, being a genie was *supposed* to be fun. And he supposed it was, for the elders, the ifrits. After all, they had access to all the real magic, the kind that could create worlds—or end them.

But for young genies like Jin, the ones the elders wanted to torture and punish until they learned *humility*, of all useless things, *they* only had a fraction of the power they'd have access to later, after their one thousand and fifty years of service.

And given that he'd only been "born" twelve years ago, Jin still had a *long* way to go.

Not to mention that the whole service thing was absolutely filled with rules, all of which just punished good, decent, hardworking genies like Jin! Like how the human who held his specific control device—in Jin's case, a ring—could make three wishes, and Jin *had* to fulfill them, no matter how long it took, or what he had to do to make the wish come true; it was an unbreakable rule, at least at his current power level.

But not only that, the rules said that the ring bearer could also punish Jin if he misbehaved in any way . . . but didn't ever say what misbehaving even *was*! So if you had a horrible human holding your control device, like, say, *the Golden King*, he could punish you for doing just about anything he didn't like, and apparently the ifrits were totally okay with that.

Completely. Un. *Fair.*

It also didn't help that Jin was the first new genie in a few millennia, so the ifrits were being extra careful around him, not giving him access to any good magic. In fact, all he could really do was change his own body however he wanted— magic inherent to every genie—and teleport himself wherever he wished.

And that was *it*. So much for the all-powerful genies!

Granted, the elders *claimed* they had their reasons. Apparently the last genie they'd tried to teach humility had just faked it, then almost destroyed the entire universe over some issues with a mirror and a fairy queen or two. So now Jin was stuck beneath the thumb of this golden dictator, punished whenever he was even the slightest bit snarky, and all because some genie had a temper tantrum.

Basically no one suffered like Jin, and the ifrits needed to feel sorry for him and therefore change the rules so he could have all their power early. There was no other option.

He did at least have something else going for him: knowledge. Big, cosmic knowledge that could tell him the age of a star or how long it took for a diamond to form beneath a dragon, given the proper materials.

But again, the elders, in all *their* wisdom, didn't want him figuring out how to use that knowledge to access the magic that was *his birthright* early, so they'd restricted his access to the knowledge, too! At least it was all still available, just in a much more annoying way.

"All I'm asking is where I can find this Last Knight person," Jin said, floating around in the Golden King's personal chamber, the king now having gone to turn the various nobles—as well as the guards who'd seen his humiliation—into golden statues. Jin figured the Last Knight had probably found his own way in and was just causing chaos by suggesting the nobles had done it, something Jin could appreciate. But considering the king wouldn't let anyone see him embarrassed, that might not have even mattered. "It shouldn't be that hard!"

Oh, it wouldn't be, the cosmic knowledge said in his head, *not if you had your full power. But that would hardly teach you humility, would it?*

Jin gritted his teeth, the ones he only had so that the humans wouldn't find out their king had access to a genie. "Where is *your* humility, huh? I don't hear you talking about how we should all be peaceful trees or something!"

Is that really what you think humility is? Maybe we need to start with definitions.

Jin let out a frustrated growl. "You helped me on the first wish, didn't you? What's changed?"

For the first wish, we told you about the series of difficult tasks it would take to fulfill the wish, and you—

"Succeeded in every single one!" Jin said.

Ignored us, and instead fulfilled the Golden King's wish with a series of clever, if completely immoral, tasks, the cosmic knowledge continued.

"Oh, look who's suddenly so judgmental, just because they know everything in the universe," Jin said, rolling his eyes as he flopped down onto a long, thin couch that turned out to be even more uncomfortable than it looked. "I got him voted into the chancellorship, and that's what he wished for. And all I had to do was start a few rumors, spy on a few people, and generally cheat in every way I could."

None of which exhibited any humility whatsoever.

"Oh, I'm *so* sorry. How exactly was I supposed to do *that*?"

By admitting that the task was beyond you and you needed help.

"I asked *you* for help!"

But you could have asked any number of humans, fairy queens, elves, dwarfs—

Jin waved his hands. "All right, enough, I get it. So if I ask for help this time, you'll see that I'm incredibly humble and give me all my magic, then? That's all I need to do?"

No, young Jin, the cosmic knowledge said. *To know you are humble, we must see you put someone else before yourself. If you wish to be free of service before your one thousand and fifty years are up, you must perform a truly selfless act.*

"A *what*?" Jin shouted. His voice must have been louder than he thought, as a guard opened the door and looked around, then shut it, but not before giving Jin an odd glance. "A what?" he said more quietly now. "There's no such thing! Even if I tried

44

to do something selfless now, you'd know I was just doing it to get my magic!"

Put others before yourself, and you will see that selflessness is not only possible, but perhaps a way to find a new *kind of magic—*

Jin gagged, shaking his head. "If you tell me that love or friendship is the real magic, I'm going to set fire to this whole world. Fine! Selfless act. I'll be on the lookout for one. Now will you help me with this wish? I have to complete this one *and* a third before I get my freedom, because someone thought *three* wishes was a much better idea than just one."

Go to the Cursed City, as the Golden King said. You will find everything—and everyone—you need there to fulfill his wish.

Jin blinked. "Oh, *thank* you for being so helpful! I thought my cosmic knowledge might be able to tell me where exactly to find this Last Knight, but no, you shared the one piece of information I already had. Incredibly useful!"

The knowledge went silent for a moment, then sounded like it coughed. *It* may *be that this Last Knight is somehow . . . eluding us. I'm finding it difficult to locate him, in fact.*

Jin's eyebrows shot up. "He's *what*? How could some human hide from all the knowledge in the universe?"

That . . . would be a good question to ask him. There are ways,

45

powerful enchanted items, some of which were well known on this world. There's something called the sword of an Eye that could potentially hide him. It would be a translucent sword, with a sort of glowing white light inside, just like the one that the Last Knight—

"*Ugh*, of course a human thought to put a hiding spell in a random sharp object," Jin said, shaking his head. "They're all just so angry and violent. Anyway, I don't need any more excuses. I'll just have to find him myself instead of asking for help, like a *humble* person does, but sure, I'll go to the Cursed City, and maybe go door to door until he shows up. Because why have all the knowledge in the world when it's easier to just ask everyone if they've seen a guy."

Perhaps you should keep in mind that the Last Knight implied the Cursed City would be hard to find.

"Perhaps *you* should keep in mind that one of the few magical powers the ifrits let me have is to teleport places," Jin said, shaking his head. "So I don't need to *find* it—I just need to magic myself there."

Again the cosmic knowledge went silent for a moment, then changed the subject, which made sense, since Jin had just outwitted it about the Cursed City thing. *Remember, young genie, that while you might not be in any danger, your actions can*

hurt those around you. Be mindful of not only the one you serve,
but the other—

"Yeah, yeah, the other humans, got it," Jin said, nodding quickly. "You act like I set fire to all the other candidates for the chancellorship or something. Only some, and none of them were even permanently hurt!" He frowned. "Well, that one wooden guy lost a toe, but that was only because he *ran* from the dragon, when he wasn't supposed to. Dragons can't resist a hunt, everyone knows that."

The voice in his head sighed. Not a great sign from the sum total of all cosmic knowledge.

Just try not to mess this up, please? Your actions could doom this
entire world, Jin.

Jin rolled his eyes. "Okay, enough. I'm just going to teleport to this Cursed City place, wherever *that* is, find this human, and carry him back here. Should be easy enough even without your help."

Not waiting for a response, Jin used his magic to teleport to the Cursed City, disappearing in a burst of smoke.

When the smoke cleared on the other end, Jin expected to find himself in the middle of a city, most likely cursed, with buildings, people, the regular sorts of city things.

But there *was* no city here, wherever he was. Instead, he found himself in the middle of a clearing, surrounded by dozens of knights in full armor, their helmet visors open . . . and empty.

The Faceless. No one knew what they were, or how empty armor could move around on its own, but they were legitimately the creepiest—and most feared—soldiers of the Golden King.

And now here they were, all aiming their black swords at Jin.

How'd the teleporting go? the cosmic knowledge asked. *Did it work just as you thought it would? Everything go as planned? Is this the city?*

Oh, be quiet, Jin thought, then turned to the Faceless. "Well, hey, look at all of you, having no faces and everything. So, um, anyone seen a Cursed City around here?"

CHAPTER 7

Getting around the village in the clouds was so strange at a regular giant's height. Lena was used to running around on Rufus's back, using his magical Seven League Boots to jump them whatever distance they wanted to go without being seen, sneaking around and watching the other giants go about their regular lives, which always resulted in feelings that were a combination of fascination and jealousy.

But from this height, everything looked off. Other houses were now small enough to live in, instead of mountains on each side of the street. The other giants were now Lena's height, instead of too tall to make out anything beyond their shoes. Even the dogs and cats in the village now looked like Rufus had when she'd shrunk him, instead of potential dangers—the dogs all still liked her at her usual size, of course, but sometimes they didn't know their own strength when they'd lick her right off Rufus's back.

The local cats were another story, and Rufus had to outrun more than one using his boots.

Mostly, though, what was strangest was how beautiful the village was from this height. Everything was designed to look nice from eye level, not from around the top of a blade of grass. The decorations in windows, the painted doors and elaborate designs of the houses, all were new and beautiful in a way Lena forgot when she was her regular size.

It reminded her of the human city on the ground directly below the giant village in the clouds, except in the human city, Lena's size was *everyone's* size, and she didn't have to hide how she looked. So no matter how beautiful her home village might be, she still didn't feel like she belonged.

But that was all going to change after the ritual.

As they walked (and Lena kept having to look down at her feet to marvel at how far her steps took her), other families began to file in around them, and a few had kids Lena's age, or close enough not to matter. She flashed the ones she'd met before a shy smile, hoping they wouldn't ask many questions about why they never saw her except on special occasions.

A few waved back, and a warm feeling spread through Lena's chest. It'd taken her twelve years to get to the ritual, but it was finally going to pay off, and she was going to have actual giant *friends*!

Her village surrounded the enormous castle of the giant king, which was the destination of several giant villages from around the clouds. From this height, Lena could actually make out the patched holes where supposedly humans had climbed enormous bean plants to steal from the last giant king, but Lena figured those were just tall tales.

What kind of bean plant grew this high off the ground? No, the only way up would have been by mountain, and the closest one was miles away. But most unbelievable of all was how the story ended, with the giant king, Ferdinand the Enormous, chasing a human thief down to the ground, only to be defeated.

Defeated by a *human*.

A tiny human about as big as the sole of the giant's boot.

Nope, there was no way. And besides, most of the humans in the village below had no idea there were giants living above them, except for Mrs. Hubbard and the Last Knight, of course, both of whom Lena had shared her secret with.

King Denir, Ferdinand's younger brother, told the story of

his brother's death by humans often enough at gatherings that even Lena had managed to hear it, both by listening secretly at her usual size and on the rare occasions she wore the Growth Ring and was allowed out in public. King Denir used the story to go on and on about what horrible, thieving, murderous creatures humans were.

But considering Lena had met more than a few humans, and found them friendly and non-murderous, she couldn't believe the story had any truth to it, no matter how often King Denir told it.

As they reached the back of the line of giants leading into the castle, Lena's mother pulled her to the side of the path and out of earshot of the assembling giants. Her father noticed too late to stop and got swept inside the castle's gate along with the rest of the mob, waving helplessly back at them.

"Okay, what are you planning?" her mother asked, giving Lena a long stare.

Lena's heart began racing. "Nothing!" she said quickly. "I'm just really excited to be coming to the ritual for the first time!"

"There's something up, I know it," her mother said, looking even more suspicious now. "Well, either way, you're staying at the back of the castle's great hall with me, and you are *not* to participate in the ritual, no matter what."

Instead of racing, her heart almost stopped at this. "*What?* But that's the whole point of coming! I'm old enough, and was invited!"

"I don't care," her mother said. "The Spark is pure magic, and if you touch it, who knows how it would mess with your Growth Ring. You might change back to your regular size. We can't take that chance."

Lena's eyes widened as she couldn't believe what was happening. "You've told me that the Spark is *healing* magic, and it keeps giants healthy and living for centuries. It wouldn't affect my ring!"

"I'm not willing to take that chance," her mother said, crossing her arms. "You're here to *see* the ritual, nothing more." Seeing the horror on Lena's face, she sighed. "And when we go home, I'll make your favorite pumpkin pancakes, okay? *If* you're good."

Lena could feel her face begin to heat up, and she bit the inside of her mouth. All her waiting, all her dreams of getting to live like a normal giant, and now her mother was going to stop her, right before it all happened? "This isn't right!" she said finally. "Why do you keep trying to *hide* me?"

A few nearby giants looked over as Lena's voice got louder, and her mother waved at them, then turned back to Lena, her own face now red as well. "This is for *your* safety, young lady," she growled. "Why can't you see that?"

"It's *not* for my safety," Lena said, glaring at her mother. "It's because you're *embarrassed*. Embarrassed that I'm not normal!"

Her mother drew back like she'd just been slapped, then narrowed her eyes. "I'm going to pretend you didn't just say that," she hissed. "But we're going to have a *very* long talk when we get home. And no pumpkin pancakes!"

"You think I care about pancakes?" Lena said, practically yelling now, and more giants turned to look. "Make your rules—I don't even care anymore. I'm not a coward. *Real* giants face what they're afraid of and stomp it right into the ground! *Giants fight to show their might!* I'm *going* to participate in the ritual, touch the Spark, and get my name like every other giant my age. And if you try to stop me, you'll just have to explain to the whole castle *why*! So let's see who's actually afraid here."

And with that, she turned and slipped past the line into the castle, where the crowd was so thick she managed to leave her mother behind, uselessly calling Lena's name.

"Hey, I saw you cut the line!" an older giant shouted as she went.

She pushed him lightly out of the way, knocking him into the nearby castle wall hard enough to shake it, and the other giants immediately made room for Lena, her face burning like the sun. How could her mother be so cruel? This was all she'd wanted since she could remember, just being a normal, regular giant. And to take it away when it was all so close? What kind of monster did that?

This is for your safety, she heard her mother's voice say in her mind. But that was ridiculous. What possible danger would the other giants be, no matter what they found out? She was one of them, not some dangerous human, no matter how much she might look like one!

The farther she went into the castle, the less she could hear her mother calling her name, and soon she decided her mother must have given up and followed. But that didn't matter. She'd find her father somewhere in the great hall, the only room big enough to contain the giants from several villages. And there he was, saving two seats near the back, one for her and the other for her mother, who still hadn't managed to make her way in yet.

"I thought I lost you two," her dad said, then looked back over his shoulder and realized it was only Lena standing there. "Where's your mom?"

"She's too embarrassed by me," Lena said, her eyes locked on King Denir, an older giant who managed to look imposing, in spite of his shorter height, by standing on a platform above them all. He wore an elaborate cape and clothes, far richer than any other giant's, and looked impatient as he waited at the front of the great hall for everyone to be seated. The Spark itself shone in a tiny, human-sized bowl on a pedestal next to the Sparktender, a giant named Creel, himself dressed in long, flowing gray robes. "She's hiding in the back, not sure if she'll make it."

"What a joker, your mom," her dad said, barely listening.

Lena glanced behind her and spotted the top of her mother's hair above the crowd. She'd find her way to their seats before the ritual started, which meant she'd be able to stop Lena from going through with her plan. Lena turned back forward, frantically looking for another seat, only to see an open one right in the front row.

Perfect.

"Be right back," she told her dad, then stood up.

"Okay, but don't take long," he said. "The ritual's about to start!"

She just grinned at him, then left to grab the last seat in the front. Soon she'd be an official member of the village, and everyone would know exactly who she was. Finally, her parents would learn there was nothing to worry about.

And would Lena love to see the look on her mother's face when *that* happened.

CHAPTER 8

The Faceless stared at Jin in silence, or so he assumed, since he wasn't sure if they could even speak or not. Either way, they weren't answering his question about the Cursed City. Unless pointing their swords *was* their answer, he supposed.

"We don't really need those, do we?" Jin asked, reaching out to push one of the swords away. "We all work for the Golden King—"

The moment he touched the blade, though, he screamed in pain and immediately yanked his hand back as his body abruptly felt weak. His knees began to buckle, and little spots began exploding before his eyes. What was going on? No earthly weapon should be able to hurt him, not his true self. What kind of magic did these things *have*?

"**You are not human,**" one of the Faceless said, its voice an echoing chorus, as if the empty armor reflected it over and over. A skittering noise like insects erupted as each of the Faceless moved closer, and Jin quickly put up his hands in surrender.

"No, I'm not!" he said, watching the nearest sword nervously. "But I'm on your side! The Golden King, he told me to come here. And you answer to him too . . . right?"

The Faceless didn't respond and just moved in closer, forcing Jin to flinch away from the blades. He tried to reach out with his senses to figure out what these weapons were and how they could do . . . whatever it was that they'd done to him, but somehow his innate magic just seemed to disappear when he turned it on their swords.

Hey, cosmic knowledge, what is going on *here?* he shouted in his head.

Oh, interesting! the reply came, making Jin wince. Whenever the cosmic knowledge found something interesting or fascinating, it always seemed to end badly for him. *Those swords are made of shadow magic. Don't touch one.*

Don't touch *one?* Jin screamed at the voice. *I might not have a choice in the matter! Is that really the best information you have for me?*

59

Shadow magic grows in power by absorbing regular, natural magic. You know, the stuff you're made of.

Oh great*!* Jin shouted in his mind, then turned back to the Faceless. "Really, I'm just looking for the Last Knight. I'm supposed to capture him. That's probably what you're here to do too, right? All of us under orders from the Golden King?"

The Faceless closest to him leaned in. **"We do seek the Last Knight and the Cursed City,"** he said, that same, echoing voice even creepier up close. It was almost like the armor was full of creatures, all speaking at the same time. Except from the empty helmet, that didn't exactly make sense either. Were they spirits as well, like Jin? **"But we have been told nothing of you, genie. If you cannot prove the Golden King sent you, we will follow our standard orders concerning nonhuman creatures."**

Standard orders? The Golden King *had* banned all the elves, dwarfs, and other magical creatures, claiming they were a danger to ordinary humans. Did that mean he'd sent his Faceless armies after them? Just when Jin thought the king couldn't get any worse, he went and did something like that. "I can prove I work for him! What do you want to know? I was the one who won him the chancellorship! Ask me anything!"

The skittering noises came back as the Faceless straightened up. **"What is the Golden King's true name? Only his trusted servants are allowed such information."**

Right, his name! Jin almost laughed in relief. His name. The Golden King's name. The one he'd introduced himself to Jin with, before he started calling himself the Golden King, back before winning the chancellorship.

His name. *His name.*

Jin sighed deeply, wanting to punch something. How could he have forgotten the king's *name*?

Because you were barely paying attention and didn't really care, the cosmic knowledge provided helpfully.

Okay, that's on me. So tell me his name, then! You must know it.

That's right, I do, the knowledge said. *But that's no way for you to learn a lesson.*

Jin growled in frustration, only to freeze as the swords pushed in closer. "Sorry, just going through my memories of when we first met!" he said quickly. "I definitely remember it starting with a *D*."

The skittering noise returned, and the Faceless all drew their swords back, ready to strike. **"That is incorrect."**

"No, wait!" Jin said, holding his hands up to protect himself, not that it'd make any difference. "I know he said it was *D* something. Dis! He called himself Dis!"

The Faceless looked at one another, then attacked, driving their swords toward him.

"'My name is Dis,' he said!" Jin shouted, leaping backward. His foot slammed against a rock, sending him tumbling to the ground, where he quickly covered his face with his arms, hoping that if he did have his magic stolen, at least it wouldn't be painful. "Or maybe without the 'name' part? My-Dis? Was *that* it?"

The nearest shadow blade stopped just inches from Jin's face. After a moment to make sure they really weren't going to drain his magic, Jin dropped his arms again to find the Faceless returning their horrible death swords to their scabbards.

"His name is Midas," the closest one said. "You appear to have his trust. And a poor memory."

Jin almost wanted to cry, he was so happy. "That's so true! I have the worst memory in the world. But you're totally right, it *was* Midas."

Lucky guess, the cosmic knowledge said.

Oh, like you were such a help.

"Well, now that we're all allies," Jin said, standing up and dusting himself off, "what say we go find this Cursed City and this Last Knight person, so the king doesn't turn us all into gold statues?"

All of the Faceless turned away now, except the one that had been addressing him. **"There is an old, deep magical spell protecting the Cursed City,"** the Faceless said. **"Only those with no ill intent toward its inhabitants can find it. All others will be turned away, without even realizing it."**

Jin's eyebrows shot up. "Oh really? So you'd be walking toward it, then find yourself back in the place you started, that kind of thing?"

"We have searched for the Cursed City for days, yet are no closer to reaching it," the Faceless told him, and Jin almost felt sorry for the creepy, insect-sounding creatures. Almost.

"I bet *I* can find it!" Jin said, nodding confidently. "After all, I don't have any ill intent. Not toward anyone. Not toward *you* walking horrors, or the annoying, arrogant humans that seem to cover this world like some kind of fungus, *no one*. It shouldn't affect *me* at all." He started walking down the closest path, only to stop. "Is this the way?"

The Faceless lifted a hand and pointed in the opposite direction.

"Right," Jin said, and strode off down the path the Faceless had pointed out.

A few moments later, he found himself back in the clearing, the Faceless looking at him expectantly.

"Huh," he said, frowning. "Maybe I have more ill will than I thought! This *might* be a problem."

CHAPTER 9

Welcome, everyone," King Denir the Raging declared, a sparkling ring of gold around his head and a luxurious cape of purple covering up the rest of his finery. He spread out his arms toward the assembled townsfolk in the grand hall. "Welcome to our sacred Ritual of the Spark, where the children of our villages will take their first steps toward adult gianthood! Please make room for all, if you can."

Lena rubbed her sweaty hands on her pants and glanced back to see if her mom had made it any farther in. She saw two teenage giants sit down next to her father in the seats he'd been holding for Lena and her mom. Her dad started to say something, then just shrugged. Apparently her mother was going to be stuck in the back. This was working out almost too well.

"Let us begin," the king said, and gestured for the Sparktender, Creel the Wise, who stepped forward, nodding at the assembled giants. He picked up the bowl that held the Spark and raised it high.

"My friends," Creel said, looking up at the Spark. "We giants were entrusted with the Spark of Life many centuries ago, to protect it and its healing powers from those who would use its magic for evil—"

"Humans, in other words," the king said, a disgusted look on his face.

"And to use it to ensure our good health," Creel continued, lowering the Spark and holding it in front of his chest. "The Ritual of the Spark was established when we lost King Denir's brother—"

"Murdered by those filthy earthbound creatures!" the king said, spit flying from his mouth.

"To unify the various giant tribes within the clouds," Creel finished. "As the Spark represents the fire of life within us, it is only right that its power heals and renews us, giving giants the long life we currently enjoy."

"And signifies the burning *hate* we have for the thieving humans," the king said, and Lena heard Creel sigh quietly.

He glanced down at her with a sad frown, then looked away quickly, making Lena nervous. Did Creel . . . know?

But he was the one who'd sent out the invitations. If he had a problem with her real size, why ask her to come to the ritual?

"And so, as our children will one day become the elders in our tribe, let us welcome them now and grant them the same responsibility we share, to protect and cherish the Spark, the symbol of our power," Creel said, then smiled at the crowd. "After which, I understand there will be plenty of food and celebration, so let's do this quickly and get to the fun part."

The crowd laughed. "Now," Creel said, "would the children of appropriate age please step forward?"

He moved aside to make room as the other twelve-year-olds began to line up. Sitting so close, Lena managed to snag the first place in line and couldn't help but grin nervously at Creel as she waited.

As the line formed, Lena heard her name called out in a whisper from somewhere in the back. She turned and threw a quick look over her shoulder to find her mother gesturing at her frantically, shaking her head violently. But Lena just smiled in return, knowing there wasn't much her mother could do to stop her at this point, barring making a huge scene.

"And so, the time of the ritual is here," Creel said, nodding at her to step forward. "Children of the clouds, please touch the Spark's flame, and let it burn any sickness or ill health from your body. And then I shall bestow upon each of you the true name that will—"

"Hold, please, Sparktender," the king said, and Creel froze, then bit his lip, slowly turning to look at Denir. Lena did the same and found that the king had locked eyes on her, and not in a friendly, inviting sort of way. In fact, he was glaring at her with such hatred that she felt her knees start to buckle.

"Your Majesty?" Creel said. "Is there a problem?"

King Denir stepped forward, pushing almost dismissively past Creel to stand just before Lena. Even shorter than other adult giants, the king still towered over Lena, especially standing on the raised platform before her.

"*You,*" he said, his eyes burning with anger. "You are not welcome here. Who invited you?"

Lena's mouth dropped open, and she struggled to think of an answer. This was not part of the plan, not at all! "The, ah, Sparktender . . . we got an invitation," she managed to say, her voice just barely loud enough for the king to hear. "My name . . . was on it?"

"She is of the age, Your Majesty," Creel whispered. "And the law says that all giants will be welcome—"

The king sneered at Creel. "This one is *no giant*," he hissed, then stabbed a finger into Creel's chest. "And I shall deal with *you* later. You knew this . . . *creature* was not allowed to participate in such a sacred ceremony."

Creel's eyes flashed between Lena and the king, only for him to lower his head. "I apologize, Your Majesty. The mistake was entirely mine. The girl is innocent of any wrongdoing."

Every muscle in Lena's body was clenched, and part of her wanted to turn and run, just to get away from whatever was happening. The king didn't want her here, and he was looking at her like she was some sort of disgusting bug.

But giants did not *run* from danger. *Giants fight to show their might.* And Lena was nothing if not a true giant.

"I deserve to be here, Your Majesty," she said, her voice raspy in her bone-dry throat. She said it so quietly that she wasn't sure the king could even hear and started to repeat herself, only for Denir to shake his head.

"You don't even deserve to live in the clouds," he said, his eyes narrowed in rage. "Look at you, hiding your shame. But I know the *real* you, creature. And if not for your parents, I'd have thrown you down to the earth where you belong, with the rest of the filthy monsters."

Lena gasped, and she found it impossible to breathe.

"I'm . . . a giant, Your Majesty," she whispered. "Just like you."

The king leaned forward, and a wave of horrible breath crashed over her. "You are *no* giant," he whispered back. "You are a mistake, and one that continues to live here with your betters because of my mercy. And now you pretend to be a regular giant, using some temporary magical ring? All that does is hide your true nature." He sneered. "Now get out, and never come back to my castle, or I'll throw you down to the world below *myself*. Do you understand me?"

"Your Majesty—" Creel started to say, but a glare from the king silenced him instantly.

Lena turned to the giant kids around her, barely able to understand what was happening. But each of the others just looked away. Her father was watching her with a confused expression, while in the back, her mother seemed like she might cry or punch someone, maybe both.

Lena turned back to the king, who didn't look like he was going to wait much longer for a response.

Fight this! a part of her shouted in her mind. *True giants* fight! *Prove to the king, to* everyone, *that you're no different from them!*

"Get . . . *out*," the king hissed, and pushed her backward.

The crowd gasped as she slammed into the giant kid behind her, and Lena had to run the back of her hand over her face to cover her tears.

"I'm . . . I'm sorry," she said, shaking her head.

"You're sorry . . . what?" the king asked.

"I'm sorry, *Your Majesty*," she said, then bowed low, turned, and ran toward the exit.

"Lena!" her mother shouted as she passed, reaching out for her, but Lena couldn't bring herself to stop, not with the eyes of all the other giants on her. She burst out of the castle's front gate, tears freely falling now, then turned back for just a moment, hoping that maybe the king had changed his mind.

But instead, the ritual had continued without her, and the giant child who'd been standing behind her was now touching his hand to the Spark.

"Lena!" she heard her mother yell, following her out. But Lena couldn't bear to see her, talk about any of this, not now.

Instead, she ran, the king's words echoing in her head.

You knew this . . . creature *was not allowed to participate in such a sacred ceremony.*

I'd have thrown you down to the earth where you belong, with the rest of the filthy monsters.

You are no *giant.*

You are a mistake.

YOU ARE *NO* GIANT.

CHAPTER 10

"Okay, I can do this," Jin said, as the creepy Faceless knights began making their way out of the clearing in several directions. "I'm not going to let some ridiculous magic spell beat me."

You're made *of ridiculous magic spells,* the cosmic knowledge said in his head, and he snorted.

I'm made of amazing, clever *magic spells.*

And you wonder why we think you need some humility.

Okay, that was a bit fair. But also, the all-knowing cosmic awareness in his head could use a little humiliation too, which meant he *had* to figure this out.

Jin began pacing around in a circle as he thought, then hovering as he moved, when walking became too tiring.

The spell turned away anyone with ill intent, according to

the Faceless. Maybe he could trick it by, say, pretending to be looking for the Last Knight to help the man?

He paused in his pacing and concentrated hard. "This is for the Last Knight's own good," he whispered, trying his best to believe it. "Really. I have nothing but *good*will toward everyone in the Cursed City. I wouldn't even call it that, a cursed city, because that seems rude. I'm sure everyone in this *blessed* city is very nice and extremely uncursed!"

Satisfied, he set off on a path out of the clearing, completely positive that he'd shortly arrive at the city gates.

Instead, he arrived back in the now-empty clearing and began cursing in genie.

Perhaps you'd like some help? the cosmic voice said.

Oh, *now* it wanted to help? After watching him fail? No way, he hadn't even *begun* to fail yet. *No thanks, I've got this.*

It's just that there are loopholes that would allow you to find the way—

Jin shook his head. *I know the way. That's not the problem. It's the spell!*

Perhaps the spell might be negated if you were with someone who knew how to enter the city? Who bore no ill will themselves?

Jin narrowed his eyes, annoyed about all of this. "You know

what?" he said out loud. "I just thought of something. What if I find someone who knows the way and doesn't bear the city any ill will? They could probably take me in. So that means I've figured this out, all on my own!"

Who are you talking to?

"No one!" Jin shouted, his irritation growing. He closed his eyes and reached out with his senses, quickly trying to find . . . well, anyone who wasn't a Faceless. He did sense some of the latter at first, which was odd, because it felt like there were many, many more of them than it'd looked like when he'd first arrived. Were there other platoons of Faceless in the surrounding woods? Probably. The Golden King wasn't taking any chances.

But finally, *finally*, he sensed something new: a lone creature, human or close enough, all by itself in the woods not too far away. The Faceless hadn't found it yet, but they would. So really, Jin would be doing this creature a favor by helping him get back to the Cursed City. Take that, ill will!

He immediately teleported close enough to the creature to reach it quickly, but not so close that it'd see him appear, then strode off in the right direction, quietly hoping that he wasn't near enough to the city for its magic to turn him around before he found whoever it was.

Apparently the city's protective spell didn't reach this far, as a moment later, he found his target, high up in a tree, of all places.

Only it wasn't human. And it didn't look like any other creature Jin had ever seen.

"Hello?" Jin said, staring up into the branches at a small brown nest of twigs and leaves.

At first there was no response, and Jin started to wonder if he should just break his disguise and float up to look in the nest. But gradually he began to see a bright white oval appear over the top of the twigs, followed by two tiny eyes.

"There you are!" Jin said, waving, and the tiny eyes and white oval disappeared back into the nest, only to reappear a moment later with a sigh.

"Halt!" the egg shouted, its shell splitting in half to form a mouth as it spoke. It pushed itself to a standing position, little arms and legs emerging from cracks in the shell. "Go no farther, or I shall be forced to call the guards on you!"

Jin tilted his head. "Are they all your size? And eggs?" He smiled. "There must be dozens of you."

The egg's eyes narrowed. "Everyone thinks they're the first person to ever think of that. I can't tell you how many times I've heard it."

"Sorry about that," Jin said, bowing low to show his fake sincerity. "Really. I was just lost in these woods, and hoping to find some shelter for the night."

"It's just past noon," the egg said.

"No one likes you much, do they?" Jin said, then quickly shook his head. "I mean, no one likes you as much as they *should*. Why did they stick you all the way out here?"

The egg puffed itself up, making tiny cracking noises as its shell threatened to split around it. "I am one of the Cursed City's *guards*, if you must know. I'm keeping silent watch over the area as we've heard rumors of increased Faceless activity. People are getting worried that they've found a way in."

"Oh, don't worry about that!" Jin said. "I just saw a bunch of them wandering around lost. But I'm glad to tell your superiors in the city what I saw. We should go now, before the Faceless find us."

The egg peered down at him suspiciously. "And how do I know you're not on their side?"

Jin frowned, then pointed at his nose. "I have a face."

"And it could be the face of someone on the Golden King's side," the egg pointed out, which was fair, considering he was right.

"The Golden King?" Jin said indignantly. "I'd never serve that horrible man. Have you seen all the gold he wears? It's so tasteless."

"He's also trying to destroy us all because we harbor a bunch of rebels," the egg pointed out.

"And that, too!" Jin said. "Just as bad. But I'm sure you're no rebel, and just want to live your life in the city, which is where we should go now—"

"Oh, I'm a rebel all right," the egg said, and Jin held himself back from face-palming. "Sworn to overthrow the fake chancellor. He only won due to all the other candidates getting attacked by dragons, including the former chancellor!"

Jin winced inwardly. "I think I've heard something about that. Listen, it's not safe out here. Jump down, and I'll carry you back. If you don't trust me, just take me to whoever's in charge, and let them decide." He spread his arms wide "I'm unarmed, as you can see, so what's the harm? I just want a safe place to sleep for the night, one without any Faceless, preferably."

"Seriously, it's just past noon," the egg said. Jin resisted the urge to crack it in half as the egg pushed itself to the top of the nest, then stood there with his arms out. "But I'll take you to the Last Knight, and he can decide. Catch me, will you?"

Jin put out his arms, and the egg leapt from the nest, falling faster than Jin had anticipated. He jumped forward, trying to catch the little creature, but missed, and the egg hit the ground, cracking into several pieces.

Jin's mouth dropped open in horror, and suddenly he had no idea what to do. *I think I just killed the egg!* he thought at the cosmic knowledge.

Well, you can't make an omelet without—

"Oh, *nice catch*!" the egg said as its mouth formed on one of the larger pieces, yolk sprayed out all around it on the ground. As Jin looked down in fascination and disgust, the egg slowly pushed itself to a sitting position, leaving behind pieces of itself in the dirt. "I'm going to need your help now, which I feel like you sort of owe me, considering. Would you mind taking me to Dr. Horse? He's the only one who knows how to put me back together."

Jin just stared at the broken egg. A horse doctor. Because who else would put an egg together? This whole dimension was *so* odd.

But he hoped that having the egg with him would at least be enough to get him by the spell. Otherwise, this wouldn't be all it was cracked up to be.

CHAPTER 11

You are no *giant.*

Lena wanted to tear the words out of her head, but she couldn't, and they wouldn't stop echoing in her mind.

You are no *giant.*

And now you pretend to be a regular giant, using some temporary magical ring? All that does is hide your true nature.

You are no *giant.*

Her lungs began to burn, and she realized she hadn't stopped running since the castle. She glanced around, barely sure where she was at this height, as everything looked different, off.

And all because she was just pretending to be a regular giant.

She let loose a combination of rage and humiliation in one

scream, then drove her fists into the ground, setting off a mild earthquake through the village.

Everything she'd been waiting for was gone. All her dreams were now never going to happen, not with the king in charge.

You are no *giant.*

You are no *giant.*

The urge to run, to get away from the village, was almost too much to take. But where could she go? No other giant village would take a stranger in, especially not after they heard what the king had said about her.

There was the human city, of course. But how could she just abandon her family, her parents?

You are no *giant.*

And her parents hadn't objected, hadn't argued. No one had.

She slammed her fists down again, then wiped her arm over her face.

"Lena is okay?" she heard in her ear, and gasped, having almost forgotten about the one friend who was always on her side.

She carefully lifted Rufus down from where he sat behind her ear, then took off her Growth Ring, shrinking down to her regular size. As she did, she reached over and unbuckled his miniaturizing collar, and he quickly sprouted to his regular height as well.

"Lena is not okay," she told him, then climbed onto his back. "Lena needs to go away, Rufus. Maybe we go down and see Treats Lady?"

"Treats Lady!" Rufus said, running in a quick circle, which almost threw Lena from his back. She grabbed ahold of his fur and hung on tight as he shifted his direction, then leapt using his magical boots. A moment later, they landed outside Lena's own house, and Lena whispered for him to stop, just so she could take a look at it.

The sight of her cottage threatened to make her cry again, but she couldn't leave without a goodbye. And not being able to face her parents, this was the best she could do.

Granted, going down to the human city below wasn't much of a plan, but for now, Lena didn't know what else to do. Mrs. Hubbard always seemed to have treats on hand for Rufus, even when her cupboards were otherwise pretty bare. And right now, Lena desperately wanted to see her human friends, since both Mrs. Hubbard and the Last Knight knew her secret and didn't judge her for it.

In fact, the knight had once offered to permanently help her situation, with a magical cauldron that Mrs. Hubbard used to use in a former life as a witch. But Lena had hesitated, balked, and Rufus had instead jumped into it and grown to his current size. . . .

Wait. The cauldron. She'd been too scared to use it at the time, given that it turned anyone who drank from it into their *true* self. What if she hadn't really been a true giant? But now, what other choice did she have?

And if . . . no, *when* the cauldron turned her permanently big, not just temporarily like with the Growth Ring, the king would *have* to acknowledge that she was as much a giant as any of the others. Wouldn't he?

She directed Rufus into her room, where her dollhouse waited, then leapt from his back. "Give me a minute, okay?" she told her cat, digging her fingernails into her palm to keep the king's words from repeating in her mind. *Keep moving; don't feel it yet; just get everything you need and go. This can be fixed. The Last Knight and Mrs. Hubbard will help. Keep trying, keep* fighting, *like a real giant.*

She was already wearing her infinitely large pouch around her waist, so she concentrated on packing it full of clothing, food, and some items for trading. She couldn't imagine Mrs.

Hubbard would insist on payment for using her cauldron, but Lena wasn't going to take any chances. And if she never came back . . .

No. She'd be coming back. But for now, all the various human-sized magical items her parents had gotten for her were fair game for trading. And there were a *lot* of them.

How dare King Denir call the humans thieves, when half of the giants had human-sized enchantments around? How *dare*—

"Lena is going?" Rufus asked, tilting his head in confusion.

"Lena is going, and so is Rufus," Lena told him, patting his cheek as she decided she had enough things and left the dollhouse. Rufus trotted after her, still trying to get his brain to figure out this new wrinkle.

"You're a better giant than any of those horrible people, you know," Lena told her cat as they reached the next room, scratching behind his ears. "So yeah, we're going. But hopefully we'll be back soon, okay?" Saying it out loud brought a lump into her throat, and she forced herself not to think about her parents.

"Lena?" called a voice from outside, making Lena's insides freeze. Her mother must have run all the way from the castle.

"Cedra, I still don't understand what happened!" said her father, who apparently had as well.

"Lena, if you're there, we just want to talk!" her mother shouted again, but Lena shook her head.

"I can't stay here," she whispered in their direction, then got on Rufus's back. "Ready to go, little boy?"

"We go to get treats?" Rufus asked, turning his head almost ninety degrees around to look her in the eye.

"Yup, down the mountain, to the town below," she told him, nodding in the direction of the mountain. "As quickly as you can."

"Le—" her mother's voice came, only to be cut off as Rufus leapt toward the back door. His Seven League Boots kicked in, and a moment later Lena and Rufus reappeared instantly at the top of the mountain, having skipped over Lena's garden, the various other cottages beyond, and the forest past that.

Unfortunately, Rufus's boots wouldn't get them down the mountain to the ground below. Seven League Boots were great for going anywhere relatively flat, but the magic didn't work so well with ups and downs, so climbing down the mountain just wasn't going to work.

Fortunately, Rufus had some pretty amazing natural claws

of his own, so Lena took the boots off, tied them by their laces, then swung them on either side of her shoulder before mounting up again.

Rufus had done this enough times that he knew the trail by heart, but that didn't mean the trip was comfortable. Each time, there was a moment or two that Lena was convinced they were going to fall into some chasm, as the mountain was built almost in tiers, with deep crevices between each one. Rufus was agile enough to leap between the tiers, and *almost* never missed. But when he did . . .

Lena often wondered if cats that humans kept as pets were as clumsy as hers. She'd seen them around the Cursed City, and they acted like they were graceful as faeries dancing in the first snow, while Rufus could trip over his own feet while walking in a straight line.

But he always managed to pick himself up and pretend like his fall had never happened, something Lena was really jealous of at the moment.

"We come back soon?" Rufus said as he leapt through the hole in the clouds that the mountain's spire poked up through. It was so small that Lena figured most giants had never seen it, not unless they'd been down near the ground at her height.

But even so, they'd never have been able to fit through the cloud layer.

"I hope so," Lena said, not able to think about anything more. "And when we do, they won't be able to send me away again, because I'll be a *real* giant."

"Lena *is* a real giant," Rufus said, sounding confused, and she hugged him tight.

You are no *giant.*

Maybe not, she thought, *but I will be* soon.

"Hey, maybe Mrs. Hubbard will have some of those fish you like?" she said, trying to change the subject.

Unfortunately, all she did was get Rufus excited, and he tore down the mountain so fast he almost sent Lena falling off his back.

And since she'd heard somewhere that falling down mountains could break your crown, she held on tight as her cat careened down the hill, and toward Mrs. Hubbard's treats.

CHAPTER 12

You have no idea how many times this has happened," the broken egg said to Jin as they walked through the woods, Jin cradling the egg and its various broken shell parts in his hands. He hadn't bothered trying to scoop up the yolk but assumed that wasn't important, considering the egg hadn't mentioned it and was, you know, speaking. "And for a while, no one knew what to do about it."

"That's fascinating," Jin said, not listening. "So it's this way to the Cursed City, right?" The forest around them didn't look familiar, which seemed like a good sign, since it meant at least the misdirection spell wasn't sending them back over the same ground they'd already walked.

"Oh yeah, you're doing great," the egg said, then stuck out a tiny little hand. "I'm Humphrey, by the way. Everyone calls me Humpty, though."

Jin gave the egg his pinkie, and the egg shook it. "Nice to meet you, Humphrey."

"You can call me Humpty too!"

"No thanks," Jin said, looking all over. "You're sure we're not getting turned around by that spell?" He paused, realizing he wasn't supposed to know about that. "I mean, that's the story I heard anyway, that there's some spell that keeps people out."

The egg, Humphrey, waved a hand absently. "Oh sure, there's a spell. Got set up after some guy grew a big plant here and climbed up into the clouds. Found a giant, I guess, who chased him down, and where that giant landed, there's now a lake. That's how big the giant was!"

"Amazing," Jin said, nodding absently. "You're telling me that there are some humans that are just . . . taller? And you call them giants? Blows my mind, really."

"Well, the spell got put into place afterward, to keep the giants from wrecking anything else," the egg said. "But don't worry! You're with me, Humpty, and I can get you into the city, no problem. Especially for a friend of mine like you, *uh*, what did you say your name was?"

"Omelet," Jin said, giving the egg a long look. Humphrey's eyes widened, and then he laughed, slapping himself on his cracked shell, then groaning in pain.

"Omelet! That's one I haven't heard before. I'll call you Mel, then. Great to meet you, Mel. And thanks for taking care of me."

"Well, it's my fault you cracked, since I didn't catch you," Jin said, wondering if he'd known then how annoying the egg was, if he'd just have let it drop on purpose. "I suppose I owe you. Is this Dr. Horse close?"

"Used to be a king's surgeon," Humphrey said, and Jin closed his eyes in irritation, willing himself not to close his fists and squeeze anything remaining from the egg. "Turned into half a horse by some witch or another, but said he ended up liking it better that way. That's most of us here in the Cursed City, people who've had run-ins with witches, wizards, dragons, you name it. But we've gotten used to our new life, and most of us actually prefer it. Some of us even asked to use Mrs. Hubbard's cauldron, which reveals your—"

Jin cut him off before he completely lost his temper. "Fascinating! Anyway, the horse guy is where again?"

"He's the only one who figured out a way to put me back together," Humphrey said, ignoring the question. "Spent *weeks* at it the first time I cracked, years and years ago." He shrugged. "That's back when I used to guard the walls of the city. Fell every few days or so!"

"People lining up to push you, I'd imagine?" Jin asked.

Humphrey chortled, then began to cough. "Ouch! Don't make me laugh—it hurts!"

Jin immediately began thinking of every joke he knew. But before he could launch into them, a path opened up before him, a *real* path, with cobblestones and wheel ruts from wagons and everything. "Is this it?" he asked, just thankful to be able to drop the egg somewhere nearby. "Is this the city?"

"We're getting close!" Humphrey said, putting a hand up to block the sun. "Should be able to make out the walls in a moment or . . . Yup, there they are!" He pointed down the road, and Jin could just make out a tall stone wall rising above the trees. "That's the very one I fell from the first time!"

You're so close, Jin thought. *Don't crack him again. You might still get some useful information out of him. Just because you haven't yet doesn't mean it's impossible.*

You don't seem to be handling this very well, the cosmic knowledge pointed out. *Humpty is a good egg, as they say. Look at his inner light—it glows brightly!*

I think I saw his inner light when he cracked open, and it's just yolk, Jin thought back, then turned to the egg. "Now that we're getting close, I have a question for you. You know, since I'm saving your life and everything. Do you happen to know where the Last Knight is?"

The egg's smile immediately faded, and he looked up at Jin with suspicion. "And why would you want to know that?"

Jin forced himself to look guilty, as if caught in a lie. "I have to admit, I wasn't entirely truthful before, when I said I was just looking for a place to spend the night."

"I figured, since it's barely the afternoon."

"*That doesn't matter* . . . I mean, good point! What I'm trying to say is, I've been looking for the Cursed City just so I could meet the Last Knight and join the rebels." He gave the egg his most sincere expression. "There's no one I hate more than the Golden King."

That part was true, at least.

The egg seemed to consider this as the trees fell away, revealing the walls of the city, extending off to the sides of the path too far to see. Above the wall rose too many buildings to count, all looking well taken care of and lived in. How big *was* this city?

"Well, first, when I said we were all rebels, that's sort of misleading," Humphrey said, frowning. "We're supportive and all, but we're no army. All the most powerful rebels have been captured by the Golden King and turned to statues. It's basically just the Last Knight left now. I think he keeps trying to rescue them, but no luck so far."

"So he's alone." Jin paused. "Were there some twins in the rebellion?"

"Twins?" the egg said, considering this. "Not that I know of. Why do you ask?"

"Eh, not important. Where did you say the Last Knight was again?"

"Only Mrs. Hubbard knows," Humphrey said. "Can't be too careful. But I'll warn you, she's not one to mess with. She's got the largest collection of enchanted items I've ever seen. You should see some of the fun things she's got in her boot!"

"Mrs. Hubbard, boot, sure," Jin said, noticing several guards on the wall now, all much more intimidating than Humphrey, given that none of them were eggs. Instead they all looked human—or close enough to it—from a distance and were standing at attention, staring straight off over Jin's head. Each one looked almost like an exact replica of the others, their bright red clothing and black hats identical, with white hair that looked almost like wigs.

And as he and the egg approached, something else came into view. The guards had *enormous* teeth, of all things. . . .

"Nutcrackers!" Humphrey shouted out, waving at the guards. "He's with me. Can you open the gates?"

One of the guards tilted slightly from one side to another, like his body was frozen and that was the only way he could move. He must have activated a switch, though, as the wooden gates both opened out, revealing a buzz of people behind them.

"Nutcrackers?" Jin asked the egg, holding it closer to his face so the guards wouldn't overhear.

"Wooden soldiers, basically," the egg said, then shivered. "I'm not too fond of them, personally. Sometimes they get this look in their eye that they want to be cracking something, and I'm the perfect size." He waved up at the guards again, then nodded toward the open gate. "Come on, then, no time to waste. Dr. Horse typically starts napping soon, and I'd rather not wait for him to wake up to fix me."

Jin couldn't argue with that. He passed under the walls and through the gate, marveling at how many people there were inside the city, even this close to the walls. And not just humans, or at least not that *looked* human.

The egg wasn't wrong: almost everyone Jin saw seemed to suffer from some curse or another. But none of them looked particularly upset about it, including the human-sized frog that was striding around wearing a crown and long purple cape, upon which a number of regular frogs rode.

"The Frog Prince," Humphrey pointed out, sounding reverent. "Some say he helped take down the Wicked Queen the *first* time, with Snow White and the rest. Too old now to fight, so we just take care of him."

Right, so basically everyone here was useless. How the Golden King hadn't managed to take over the city was beyond Jin. "Where's this Mrs. Hubbard, then?" he asked, ready to drop the egg at the first sign of a horse.

Weirdly, a voice answered him from an empty spot just beyond the gate. "What do I look like, a map? Find it yourself."

Jin blinked, not sure what had just happened. But the egg didn't seem to have heard.

Jin squinted his eyes, looking past the visible, and found a humanlike shape formed of magic, one with almost more dark than light.

"Who's that?" he asked, nodding at the empty space. "I just heard a voice over there, but I don't see anyone." That last part was sort of the truth, as he had no idea *what* he'd just seen.

"Oh, you did?" Humphrey asked, looking surprised. "There've been rumors we're haunted by something, but most of us in the city can't see or hear it. From what I hear, it's not very nice, so I just call it the Invisible Cloud of Hate."

"Ignore me at your own peril, egg!" the voice shouted, now on a different side of Jin, who whirled around in surprise. But again, Humphrey didn't seem to have heard.

Ugh. This city was ridiculous, and Jin had a wish to grant. "We're sorry to get in your way, Invisible Cloud of Hate," he said, not sure where the cloud actually was. "But if you don't want the egg to ignore you, I'm happy to help teach him a lesson." He flicked the egg slightly, just to show solidarity, and Humphrey let out a little indignant shout.

The cloud snorted. "Oh, *you* I could get along with. See you around, genie."

Jin's eyes widened, but no one else around seemed to be able to hear the cloud either, so his secret was probably safe. Still, maybe it was time to get away from the far-too-knowledgeable

Invisible Cloud of Hate, just in case it decided to keep sharing information.

"I'm surprised you saw the cloud," Humphrey said as they reached the next street over, this one even busier than the gate had been. "Like I said, almost no one can. I thought it was just a rumor for the last few months, honestly."

"Well, I make friends wherever I go," Jin said through his clenched teeth, not liking how crowded it was here. Why did there have to be so *many* humans in the city? He could almost see the odors rising off the city's people, and they were *not* pleasant. "Mrs. Hubbard was where again?"

"Oh, you can see her house and store from here," Humphrey said, and nodded farther into town. "Those two giant boots? The ones that could literally be worn by giants? That's where she and the kids live and work." He gave Jin a worried look. "Be careful around her. Like I said, she's a tough cookie, even compared to Mr. Ralph." He pointed at a large, man-shaped cookie, racing from the gate at the front into the city, as if he had somewhere to be urgently. "And *he's* made of gingerbread!"

CHAPTER 13

Lena wasn't going to forget what happened back in her village any time soon, but seeing all her friends from the human city below did help distract her, at least.

"It's been weeks!" Mr. Ralph said, his gingerbread arms raised in the air in celebration as she and Rufus walked through the back gate to the city, unlocked by a few of the nutcracker guards standing atop the walls. They'd recognized her on sight and greeted her with their loud, clacking mouths opening and closing, while Mr. Ralph had run up out of nowhere a second later, as quick as always. How a cookie got around so fast was beyond her. "Did you get taller, Lena? I swear, you're growing like a weed."

Lena winced, not wanting to talk about her height at all. Mostly she could just laugh it off when the townspeople pointed out how tall she was for her age, since human girls at twelve were typically a good head shorter than she was. But at the moment, that was the last thing she wanted to talk about.

"How are you, Mr. Ralph?" she asked, going in for a hug. The smell of ginger filled her nose, and for a moment, everything wasn't quite so horrible.

"Oh, life is as delicious as always," he said with a grin, then turned to Rufus. "And you, big boy! Have you grown, or did you decide to stick with just being a horse-sized cat?"

Rufus started to respond, then sniffed at the air and abruptly hissed. "Something is here, Lena," he said, eyes darting back and forth. "Something is in the city with us."

She sighed adoringly at her cat, knowing that when he sniffed an odd smell, it was usually fairies, which always seemed to be around when Lena came by. Rufus loved chasing them.

"You're such a *brave* guard cat," she said, and scratched the cat's ear fondly. "Come on, let's go find Mrs. Hubbard."

Mr. Ralph said goodbye, with a promise to meet up later, then turned to run off somewhere new as Lena headed to the Boot-ique, Mrs. Hubbard's store she'd made from a giant's boot Lena had traded to her years ago. It'd been one of a pair, and the old woman had used the other to house her family, which worked out much better than it sounded.

As she and a slightly on-edge Rufus made their way through the city, Lena tried not to slow down too much, even as half the residents seemed to want to say hello. It wasn't that Lena didn't want to catch up with all of them, but right now, she needed to talk to Mrs. Hubbard about her cauldron. If Lena remembered right, its magic turned you into your true self, which for a cat like Rufus, who pictured himself as huge and intimidating, had ended up growing him.

At the time, Lena had been too nervous to try it, just not sure what the cauldron would show her. What if she *hadn't* grown, and her true self was human-sized? Or what if something even stranger happened, like she turned into a completely different object? The guard Humpty had drunk from the cauldron and morphed into an egg, which was perfect for him, since he loved bird-watching and now could do it from within a nest.

But Lena couldn't imagine life as an egg or a cookie or even a large chicken, like Lil, and so she'd turned down Mrs. Hubbard and the knight at the time.

But now she had no choice. It was either take a chance on the cauldron, or . . . or . . . well, Lena couldn't even imagine an "or." Any other possibility was just too awful.

So instead of finding out how all her friends in the city were doing, Lena had to content herself with a quick smile and a hello. At least their excitement at seeing her was soothing and almost helped distract Lena from her situation. *Almost.*

As they neared the giant-sized brown leather boot that was the Boot-ique, Lena found another old friend outside the store, this one entirely human and wearing the all-black uniform that said he was on duty, guarding the former Chancellor of the Kingdoms. "Peter, how are you?" Lena asked, beaming. She reached out for a hug, which Peter returned, smiling as well. "How's the family? Is the house still standing?"

"Yes, it is!" Peter said, laughing. "We just have to scrape the rot off the pumpkin every so often, but it's working. I can't thank you enough for giving us that magic pumpkin seed. It's the only type of house Petunia will live in." He narrowed his eyes playfully. "Still won't tell me where I can get more, will you?"

"No, that's my secret, I'm afraid," she said, not liking the reminder that many of the city's residents didn't know she was actually a giant. That had been something Mrs. Hubbard had warned her against sharing, just in case the humans took it badly, but today of all days, it wasn't helping to know that these people, her *friends*, didn't know the truth about her either. "And the kids are okay?"

"Yup, doing great, and we're growing a couple of your giant squashes for them to live in when they get bigger. Even a giant pumpkin's a bit too small for us all, you know?"

"I thought you were here to watch over me, not talk with my favorite stranger," said a monotone voice, and Lena yelped in surprise and happiness as a human-sized wooden puppet emerged from the Boot-ique, his strings neatly tied across his back in a bow.

"Chancellor Pinocchio!" Lena shouted. "I've missed you on my last few trips."

"*Former* chancellor," the puppet said, shaking his head. "I'm just like everyone else now, after the Golden King sent dragons after me so I wouldn't run for office again. I suppose I could have tried to fight them off, but . . ." His nose twitched, and he crossed his eyes to stare at it, looking a bit worried.

"How are things in the city?" Lena quickly asked to change the subject.

"They'd be better if the guards could keep their minds on their jobs," Pinocchio said with a laugh, and Peter blushed, straightening up and stepping away from the conversation to watch over them.

"Oh, everyone loves you here," said a new voice, and Mrs.

Hubbard, an older woman with white hair and a flowery dress, stepped out of her Boot-ique for her own Lena hug. "What could you possibly have to worry about, anyway?" she said to the puppet. "You were the best chancellor our land has ever had!"

"I was pretty amazing, wasn't I?" Pinocchio said with a grin, only to cringe as his nose grew an inch longer. He sighed and pushed it back into place. "Oh stop it, I was just joking. I know I was competent at best."

They all waited for his nose's reaction, but when it didn't move, Mrs. Hubbard shook her head, grinning. "*That* is why you were so loved. Even if you didn't get much done, we all knew we'd get the truth from you. What more could you want in a leader?"

"Oh, I'd love it if our *current* leader weren't trying to throw me in a dungeon and destroy this city, but I see your point," Pinocchio told her.

"Enough chitchat," Mrs. Hubbard said, waving the former chancellor to leave. "Lena and I have some catching up to do." She eyed the pouch on Lena's belt. "And maybe some trading, if I'm not mistaken."

Pinocchio and Peter both turned toward Lena greedily. "You

brought new enchanted items?" Pinocchio asked. He leaned in close. "Let me know if there's anything that could help with the rebellion. The Last Knight—"

"Is busy, as you should be," Mrs. Hubbard said, shooing them all away as if she were scatting cats. "As for whatever Lena brought, you'll see it at the same time as everyone else, when I get it on my store shelves. Now go!"

Peter and Pinocchio reluctantly left with one last wave goodbye as the old woman led Lena and Rufus into the boot, children's screams echoing from the boot's twin next door, startling a few fairies off a nearby roof and into the air. Lena had to throw an arm over Rufus's neck to keep him from chasing them.

"You'll have to go see the kids next, or they'll never forgive me," Mrs. Hubbard told Lena as she led them toward the back of the store. She pulled on a shoelace near the counter, and the front of the boot slowly closed, leaving the store lit only by some magical candles.

"I . . . don't have a lot to trade," Lena said quickly, feeling the crushing weight of the king's dismissal push down on her now that most of her friends were gone. "I'm sorry, I don't want to disappoint people, but—"

"That can wait," Mrs. Hubbard said firmly, and put a hand

on Lena's shoulder. "What happened, child? You look like you're about to fall apart."

Lena tried to laugh, but it just came out as a quiet sort of sob. "I, um, tried to participate in the Ritual of the Spark," she said. "It's when the Sparktender gives us our epithet, the name that describes our inner self, and only giants age twelve and up can participate. So this was going to be my first ritual, but . . ." She sniffed loudly, not sure she could continue.

"Oh, Lena," Mrs. Hubbard said, hugging her tightly. "Was it the king? You told me about his brother, and how much he hates humans. But what kind of horrible person would hold that against you?"

Lena nodded, not able to continue just yet. She rubbed at the wetness on her face and sighed. "I thought I might try the cauldron," she said finally. "You know, the one that reveals the truth about you."

Mrs. Hubbard winced. "I'd be happy to let you use it, but the Last Knight has it, darling. He was just here and asked to borrow it, but wouldn't say why. Something about all the Faceless searching for our city." She patted Lena on the shoulder. "I'm sure he'll be back with it soon. But are you sure you're ready to make the change? You won't know for sure what the cauldron will show until you drink from it."

Lena swallowed hard, then nodded. "I don't have a choice," she said quietly. "They . . . they don't see me as a giant, as *me*, even with the Growth Ring. King Denir . . . he said the Growth Ring was only temporary, and I'm no giant."

Mrs. Hubbard's eyes narrowed, and she began murmuring something beneath her breath in words Lena didn't understand. Various sharp tools from around the Boot-ique rose into the air, glowing with an eerie light. "I could go have a talk with him for you, if you'd like?" she asked, her eyes turning black.

"Oh, no, it's okay!" Lena said quickly, putting her hands up to stop the old woman. "And you decided to leave witching behind, so I can't have you doing it on my account!"

Mrs. Hubbard seemed to consider this, then gently lowered the tools back to their displays. "That's true," she said finally. "And I did make a promise to that handsome man and his twin children about not hurting anyone else, when they told me about this city. I'd probably regret breaking that promise. At least no one judges me for my past here!"

"They're such good people here," Lena said, considering that. She took a deep breath. "Maybe it's time for me to tell the others in the city who I really am. That might help, you know? Just to have more people know I'm a giant than you and the Last Knight?"

The old woman looked worried and turned away. "I don't know, dear. I'd hope that finding out your secret wouldn't change anything for most, if not all, of them, especially considering how . . . unusual we all are down here. But I wouldn't want you being hurt again, just in case, so please, to be safe, let's still keep that to ourselves for now."

Lena nodded, feeling the same anxious twinge she did whenever Mrs. Hubbard requested this. Did the humans really hate giants as much as giants hated them? And if so, what did that mean for someone like Lena?

At least here, in the Cursed City, she didn't have to hide her true height, not like back in the giant village. So that was different and helped.

Or so she told herself.

She dug her fingernails into her palm, trying to believe it.

"Let's move on to happier things," Mrs. Hubbard said as Rufus sniffed around the back, looking for fish. She tossed him a treat from a pouch she kept around her waist, and he leapt for it in the air, missed, and crashed into a mound of wool blankets. "I'll get you set up in the boot with us until the Last Knight comes back."

"He's not in the city?" Lena asked, raising an eyebrow. Usually the knight didn't leave, except on missions, as the Golden King could track him down without the city's misdirection spell.

"He's off in that hiding place of his with the cauldron, doing secret things," Mrs. Hubbard said with a shrug. "I'd suggest you wait for him, but . . ." She eyed Lena. "I'm guessing that won't be happening. Do you want to trade before you go?"

"Oh, I did bring *some* things for you," Lena said, digging into her own infinitely large pouch. She wasn't in the trading mood at all but didn't want to disappoint Mrs. Hubbard, either. "I grabbed what I could on my way down, but it isn't much."

She pulled out a large metal blade, which resembled a sword, only without any kind of hilt. "This was part of a magic compass," Lena said, holding it up. "My mother . . ." She paused, swallowing hard, then continued. "She said it *should* function even without the rest of the compass." Lena held up the giant arrow. "It supposedly points at whatever you need the most at the moment."

Mrs. Hubbard's eyes widened. "That could be incredibly

helpful, even just for finding lost items, if they were the thing you needed the most. Have you tried it? Does it work?"

Lena shrugged. "Let's see." She held out the blade and closed her eyes.

Show me what I need the most, she thought, images of the other giants at the ritual filling her head, even the king's enraged face. *Show me what I need to make them* understand *that we're all the same.*

The sword jumped in her hand, pulling her in a circle, until it stopped, pointing right out the door of the boot.

"See?" Lena said. "It's telling me I need something outside the Boot-ique!"

What Lena didn't hear over her own words was the tiny gasp that came from something invisible right at the end of the compass needle.

CHAPTER 14

Jin stared at the sword blade pointing directly at his invisible chest, just a few inches from touching him.

His first thought was he was glad he'd come into the boot invisibly. Running into the Invisible Cloud of Hate had given him the idea, and it'd made getting around the city much easier.

His second thought was being invisible didn't help if you gasped out loud when surprised.

After dropping the egg off with what turned out to be a centaur doctor, he'd made his way quickly over to the twin giant boots, turning translucent along the way to better hide, only to find a girl and her enormous cat talking to an older woman who he assumed was Mrs. Hubbard, along with the chancellor who he'd helped the Golden King beat in the last choosing. *That* had been a bit awkward, and he'd been thankful to be invisible the moment he laid eyes on the puppet. Not that the wooden creature would recognize him necessarily, but it wasn't a chance worth taking.

By the time he'd gotten over his shock, the girl, Mrs. Hubbard, and the giant cat had gone into the boot and closed it down. Jin had spent a few minutes trying to sneak in before just giving up and turning himself insubstantial, then floating right inside.

And that was when he found himself at the end of the girl's extremely large compass needle.

He looked up into the girl's face, hoping to figure out *some* context to this, but almost gasped again: she was looking *right* at him, straight into his eyes. There was no way she could see him, it couldn't be possible, but still, it was disconcerting.

Even weirder was the fact that his heart began beating faster.

Uh-oh, said the cosmic knowledge.

Jin frowned, not sure what it was talking about. On a whim, he looked beneath her surface level to her inner magic—

The brightness almost blinded him. The girl glowed like the *sun* on the inside, a blue light streaked with red cracks, as if she'd been through something incredibly painful. Jin's mouth dropped open at the sight. He'd never seen anything like this in his life.

Oh, wonderful, shouted the cosmic knowledge, making Jin jump. *It's her. There goes any possibility of a selfless act now. I didn't realize we were already this far along.*

Um, what? Jin thought as he quickly stepped aside. The girl put the compass needle down and went back to talking to the old woman. Her cat, though, had his eyes locked on Jin, and his whiskers were twitching. *That* could be a problem.

Don't worry about the girl for now. She's going to change everything for you, but you're better off not knowing about it now.

Okay, what is that *supposed to mean?*

"You know, maybe trading should wait," the girl said to the older woman, looking sad about something or other. "I can't stop thinking about the cauldron, so maybe I should just go get it over with and find the Last Knight."

Jin's eyebrows shot up. This girl knew the Last Knight, and where he was? Coming in here at this moment turned out to be pretty lucky!

There's no such thing as luck in this universe, the cosmic knowledge said to him. *You were always going to meet this girl. I'd just hoped to mold you into something more useful first.*

Jin rolled his eyes. *Uh-huh. Stop trying to sound important. She's probably just some random human girl, and I came in at the right moment to hear her talk about the Last Knight. Nice try, though.*

Instead of responding, the voice laughed, chilling Jin to his very bones. If he had them.

"I don't know that it's really safe, dear," the old woman who had to be Mrs. Hubbard said. "Not with all the Faceless out there. You might get caught by them before even making it to him."

Wait. After everything Jin had done, the Last Knight wasn't even in the city? *Are you kidding me?*

What were you saying about luck again?

"Oh, I'm not scared of them," the girl said, and Jin ground his teeth, wishing they'd get back to the important stuff, like where exactly the knight was. Annoyed, he found himself staring at the girl without realizing it. She was taller than he was, noticeably taller. And there was something about her face that—

Did you just raise your height? the cosmic knowledge asked.

Jin turned red. *No. You're imagining things.*

Sure I am.

Mrs. Hubbard began telling the girl horrible stories about the Faceless, but Jin's attention was pulled away by a loud sniff at his side. He turned and just about jumped out of his shoes when he found the large cat standing almost right on top of him, its ears back and a wild look in its eyes. He quickly moved out of its way, but the cat followed right along.

How could it sense him? He'd made sure his body didn't give off any sort of smell, and he was invisible to the cat's eyes. It might have heard the gasp earlier, but after that, he'd been silent. He quickly threw a look at the girl, but she didn't seem to have noticed.

Cats are inherently magical, and can sense other magic in their vicinity, the cosmic knowledge told him, sounding a bit smug.

Oh, very *useful to find that out* now, Jin responded. *Is there some way I can hide from him?*

Nope! Now the voice definitely sounded giddy.

You're enjoying this way too much.

Well, you deserve it. Also, you keep looking at the girl. Or had you not noticed?

Jin gritted his teeth, ignoring the voice as he moved again, this time closer to the girl, hoping to distract the cat with her presence. Weirdly, she smelled . . . pleasant to him, though he couldn't figure out what her scent was.

Clouds and sunshine, the voice said, and Jin wanted to vomit.

She's using some sort of magic on me. That must be why I keep looking at her, Jin thought. *Probably some sort of evil spell that's making my heart beat faster too.*

Oh yeah, that's *it, for sure. Couldn't be anything else.*

"Oh, I'll be fine," he heard the girl say, waving off whatever the old woman had mentioned about the Faceless. She grabbed the cat who had followed Jin and hugged him close. "I have Rufus to protect me."

The cat, Rufus, meowed indignantly. "There is something strange here, Lena."

Jin froze, watching the girl carefully in case he had to run. But the old woman just smiled and patted the cat.

"He already senses the Faceless," Mrs. Hubbard said. "Brave Rufus, promise me you will protect Lena?"

"I always protect Lena," Rufus said, sounding annoyed, which made sense, as Jin had used the distraction to get as far away from the cat as possible without leaving the boot.

"I know you do, dear," the old woman said. "Still, Lena, it'd be smart to wait. We've never seen their numbers in this area like we are now, and . . . oh, don't mind me, one never stops mothering, not while I'm raising ten kids."

Get back to talking about where the Last Knight is! Jin thought at them, hoping if he willed it hard enough, they'd do it. His gaze fell on the girl's face again, and he wondered why he'd never noticed that humans could be so visually pleasing before.

You think she's cute, the sum total of cosmic knowledge said to him.

I think she's going to lead me to the Last Knight, Jin thought back, but overall he felt more confused by the voice than anything. He'd never really found something "cute" before. Wasn't that reserved for young offspring of animals or humans?

That, and people you find visually pleasing.

I told you, she must have cast some sort of magical spell. I don't find any *humans visually pleasing.*

Oh right, the spell. Of course. How could I forget.

Jin rolled his eyes, then turned back to the girl, only to find something huge and furry blocking his sight. The cat got right in his way, staring Jin in the eye and licking his lips.

"Go *away*," Jin whispered at it, and waved a hand right in front of the cat's face, hoping the small breeze would scare it.

Instead, the cat's tail began twitching, and he pounced directly at Jin. The cat's weight knocked Jin off balance, and they both fell to the floor, the great animal's paws on Jin's shoulders as his enormous mouth moved in for the kill.

"Rufus, what are you doing, little boy?" the girl asked, and came over to investigate. She looked down directly at Jin, and again, as their eyes met, a strange feeling passed through him, like nothing he'd ever felt before . . . almost a jolt to his very core. Whatever spell she'd used must have been even more powerful than he thought. "Did you find something? Is it a fairy? Just let it go."

Apparently she couldn't tell from her angle that the cat's paws weren't touching the floor.

"Not a fairy," the horrible cat said, its eyes locked on Jin. "Not sure what it is."

"Okay, but don't eat it, whatever it is," Lena said, which Jin was thankful for.

Even so, he'd had enough of this. He turned himself intangible and twisted out from beneath the cat, who thumped down to the floor, then immediately smacked a paw right through his body, then again. "I lost it," Rufus said, looking back sadly at Lena.

"You're such a good boy," she told him, giving him a loving look, which made Jin want to vomit.

Humans were so odd around animals with big eyes and fluffy fur. No one would ever catch a genie calling some ridiculously furry beast a good anything. Or cute, either.

Because you're saving that for this girl.

Oh, be quiet.

"Anyway, I think I hear what you're saying," Lena said to the old woman. "But I don't know that I can wait. I'll be careful, though, and I'll let you know if it . . . if it works."

Mrs. Hubbard nodded, wringing her hands. "If it does, I have a feeling I'll know. You'll be pretty visible, even from the city."

The girl smiled back. "That's true," she said, leaving Jin with zero idea what they were talking about. She reached out to hug the old woman. "And I promise I'll avoid the Faceless if I can!"

Just as she finished saying it, a shout came from outside the boot.

"They're coming!" someone shrieked, so high-pitched it hurt Jin's ears. "The Faceless, they're *coming*!"

CHAPTER 15

Mrs. Hubbard quickly opened the Boot-ique back up, and Lena ran out to see what was happening. Rufus, though, stayed just inside the boot, peeking out to carefully assess the situation first.

Outside, a large chicken was running around, screaming at the top of her lungs. "The Faceless are everywhere! I barely made it back into the city. We're doomed. They're going to find the city and destroy it! Evacuate! EVACUATE!!!"

Others gathered, including the Frog Prince, who put his webbed hands up to calm the chicken down. "Lil!" he said. "Please keep calm. What is going on?"

"I was just talking to Humpty!" Lil clucked, her face contorted with terror. "He said he heard there were a bunch of

Faceless outside, coming for the city. Some even tried to capture a stranger he talked to! We're all *doomed*!"

The crowd began to murmur in fear, and Lena thought she heard someone next to her swear, though when she looked, there was no one there. The Frog Prince, though, turned to address the gathering crowd. "Everyone! There's nothing to worry about. The sky isn't exactly falling. I'll go question Humpty myself and see what the situation is. For now, go back to your homes, just for safety's sake—"

"You're telling us to hide?" a donkey with bags of cabbage on his back brayed. "Does that mean there's something in the city *already*?"

"Lil is right: we're all going to die!" shouted someone else.

The crowd began to scream and run in different directions, while the Frog Prince tried to keep them calm, only to have to hop out of the way of the mob as they rushed off to their homes. "You!" he shouted at Lil as the citizens dispersed. "You can't just go panicking everyone like that!"

"I'm *saving* them!" Lil clucked indignantly. "Remember the boy who cried wolf all those years ago, and no one believed him, but then the Wolf King attacked with the Wicked Queen's armies? I'm not going to let the same thing happen here!"

The Frog Prince sighed as Lil ran off shrieking her warning, then noticed Lena standing there, with Rufus at her side. "You should probably go back to . . . wherever it is you live, Lena," he told her, smiling slightly, which just looked odd on his frog face. "We are *not* in any danger, but just in case."

Lena winced, not sure how to say she *couldn't* go back, not until she found the Last Knight and Mrs. Hubbard's cauldron. She just couldn't face her parents, not after what had happened. "Is there anything I can do to help?" she asked, trying to distract herself. "Maybe I've got some magical items that would be useful." She pulled out the compass arrow and held it up. "If you want to find these Faceless people, I might be able to use this to locate them!"

Show me the biggest danger to the city, she thought, and again the arrow yanked her arm around, turning to point at . . . nothing. She heard a small scuffle of feet, and the arrow pulled to the right, matching the sound. She frowned, wondering what it was pointing at. Was the magic defective somehow?

She banged on the arrow twice, then used it again. This time, it moved her to the left, pointing at . . . another empty spot.

"I'm sorry, I thought that would work!" Lena told the Frog Prince apologetically, blushing a bit.

"You're a dear to want to help," the Frog Prince told her, "but we'll handle this. I've got the best guards in the city on the case. Why don't you take the back gate out, and come back in a day or two. We should have everything sorted by then."

He waved, then hopped off in the direction Lil had run, while Lena just watched him go, feeling even worse than when she'd arrived. The Cursed City was the one place she thought she could go and be herself, but now even they were saying she couldn't stay. Yes, it was for unrelated reasons, but at the moment, that didn't feel any better.

Still, she'd intended to go anyway, and the back gate was the closest to the Last Knight's typical hideout, so at least she could follow the Frog Prince's orders and not get in worse trouble.

Then maybe, once she grew to a real giant's size, she could come back and stomp these Faceless for the city. That might go a long way toward making the humans less afraid of giants.

"Come on, Rufus," she said, turning back to the Boot-ique where her cat was hiding, with just his tilted head poking out from the side of the boot. "It's safe—you don't have to be afraid!"

Rufus came pawing out carefully, trying to look everywhere

at once. "I am not afraid," he told her, purring confidentially. "I was being brave, lying in wait to attack bad things and protect Lena."

"That's what I meant," Lena assured him, petting his furry head. "But we need to go."

She waved a quick goodbye to Mrs. Hubbard, then leapt onto Rufus's back and set him out in the direction of the back gate. They could have used the Seven League Boots to jump to the cave where the Last Knight usually went, but Lena didn't want to scare anyone in town by just disappearing, especially now while they were nervous about being attacked.

"Come back soon, Lena," said Mr. Ralph, the guard made of gingerbread, as he opened the gate for her. It didn't matter what gate she left by, he always seemed to be there to let her out. Either the cookie could teleport, or he was a lot faster than he looked!

"I will, Mr. Ralph, and please stay safe for me!" Lena told him as the gate slammed shut, leaving her outside.

You are no giant, the king had said, right before his castle gates had slammed on her as well. The reminder made Lena feel sick.

"We go back up the mountain?" Rufus asked, padding in that direction. "Go home again? I use the Seven Lee Boos?"

"No, we're not . . . not right now, okay?" Lena said, not wanting to explain things to her cat, though she couldn't help but be charmed for the thousandth time by how he pronounced Seven League Boots. "We're going somewhere you've only been once or twice. Come on, I'll lead you there. It'll be easier than using the boots and landing in the wrong spot."

Rufus set off at a walk, with Lena pointing in the direction she wanted him to go as she tried not to think about home, up in the clouds above her. The farther they went, the more she began to worry about the cauldron as well, and what it might show her about her true self.

What if she drank from it and *shrank*? Or turned into some kind of animal, like many of the Cursed City's residents? She'd never be able to go home to her village, but worse, she'd *know* she was no giant at that point, that the king was right.

The beautiful forest all around helped distract her a bit, though oddly, she soon noticed she wasn't hearing or seeing any animals or birds. Maybe they were still too close to town?

A cold shiver told her they were passing through the misdirection spell, something Lena hadn't felt since she'd first discovered the city below the clouds so many years earlier, since usually they Seven League Booted right through it. Feeling it now almost seemed like a goodbye, the last thing she needed at the moment. She sighed, then realized Rufus had stopped in place, sniffing at the air.

"What is it?" she whispered to him as his whiskers twitched.

"Someones," he said quietly. "*Lots* of someones."

Lena slowly dismounted, letting Rufus run behind some trees in order to "protect" her, and pulled out the giant compass arrow, just in case she needed a weapon. The sides of the arrow weren't especially sharp, but the end was pointy, and at least she could use it to block a sword if she had to.

A weird skittering noise sounded in the silent forest behind her, like insects scurrying over metal, and she whirled around to find . . . no one.

"Hello?" she called out, turning in all directions.

Something clanked, and she turned again, this time finding a knight in black armor, then another, and another, and another. Soon she was surrounded by the knights, none of whom had spoken.

"Who are you?" she asked.

Slowly the knights all raised the visors on their helmets,

revealing . . . *nothing* behind them. "We are the Faceless," the knights said in unison, their voices echoing like a chorus in their suits of armor. "And we seek the Last Knight. If you help us, you shall be rewarded. Hinder us, or keep his location from us, and we will *destroy* you."

CHAPTER 16

After listening to the chicken run around screaming for just a few seconds, Jin considered teleporting her to the moon, if only for some quiet. But that would probably reveal that he was there and make fulfilling the Golden King's wish even harder.

At least the Invisible Cloud of Hate was on his side. He'd heard her imitating the chicken in a mocking voice after everything the creature had said.

Sometimes it just felt good to know you weren't alone in your opinion of people.

Anyway, he was so close to finding the Last Knight at this point! All he had to do was follow the girl and her cat, and that'd be it. So instead of throwing it all away, he did the heroic thing and let the horrible chicken go, then followed Lena out of town, still invisible.

They left through a back gate, where the man made of cookie was also waiting. He really did get around! Apparently Lena knew him too, as they said goodbye, and that was it—they were outside.

As they passed through the spell protecting the city, Jin wondered if he'd be able to teleport back into it, now that he'd been in the city once. Experimenting, he quickly traveled back to the twin giant boots within the city, then returned to the girl and her cat. *That* was something at least. No more having to hunt down Humphrey again just to make it inside.

Or maybe the spell wasn't affecting him now because the Last Knight was no longer in the city? After all, Jin really didn't care about any of the other villagers, just the knight, so he didn't bear anyone in the city ill will at the moment.

I'd call that feeling you just had toward the chicken ill will, actually, said the cosmic knowledge.

Oh, be quiet.

Hopefully it wouldn't be an issue either way, because Jin didn't plan on ever coming back. Not to this city, to this land, none of it. And he'd never see any of these people again either, which was such a relief. No more eggs, no more chickens, no more of this girl . . .

A weird pain in his chest erupted at that thought, and he frowned, pushing on the ribs there. Had he broken something? Was there a problem with this body?

It could be that you're feeling sad about not seeing the girl again, after you find the Last Knight, the cosmic awareness said.

Jin snorted silently. *It's just the spell she used on me. There's no other explanation. Besides, feeling sad wouldn't cause pain.*

You're not used to having a human body. You have no idea what kind of power your emotions can have.

Well, *that* sounded ominous. But regardless, it wasn't like the knowledge of the entire universe knew *everything*, right? It had to be exaggerating. And if it didn't know everything, it probably had no idea about why Jin would be feeling a weird pain in his chest, like an emptiness that wouldn't go away at the thought of not seeing . . . this *town* again.

And anyway, why would he even care about . . . the town? He'd just met it. And in spite of what the cosmic knowledge said, you couldn't feel a connection to a town you just met, no matter how it felt when you locked eyes with the town, almost like you were drowning.

That probably happened with most people when they went to new, strange towns. Some weird human thing.

Oh, you're in so much trouble, Jin, the cosmic knowledge said, laughing again, and Jin smacked the side of his head in annoyance.

Ugh, why had she had to cast her magic on him? It was making this whole thing a lot more difficult than it needed to be!

Lost in thought, Jin almost walked right into the backside of the cat, who'd stopped abruptly, his whiskers twitching wildly.

"What is it?" Lena whispered to him.

"Someones," the cat replied. "*Lots* of someones."

Jin's eyes widened as he realized the cat was right. Even before he heard their insect scratching, he knew the Faceless had found them. They must be stopping anyone they found to question them, whether they knew where the Last Knight was or not.

And if the girl tells them first, the Faceless might get to him before you do. And then you won't get credit for granting your wish.

Jin gritted his teeth. Fan*tastic*. The cosmic knowledge was right, probably for the first time ever. If the Faceless got to the Last Knight first, and brought him back to the Golden King, then Jin would still owe two wishes. And that meant he'd have to go through all of this again, not to mention that the king hoarded everything of value, including wishes, so it could be years before he made another one.

No, there was no way he could let the Faceless hurt Lena. Or, uh, question her. Right. That was the important thing, that they not question her. So she could lead him and him *alone* to the Last Knight. Exactly. That was all he cared about.

You're just in so *much trouble.*

"Who are you?" Lena asked as the Faceless emerged from the woods, surrounding them.

Slowly the knights all raised the visors on their helmets, revealing the same creepy nothingness, which now was more of an annoyance to Jin than anything. What was of a lot more interest were the black swords on their belts. Whatever shadow magic was, it *hurt*, and he wanted nothing to do with it.

"We are the Faceless," the knights said in unison, their voices echoing in their armor. **"And we seek the Last Knight. If you help us, you shall be rewarded. Hinder us, or keep his location from us, and we will *destroy* you."**

Well, that confirmed it. He'd just have to save Lena and her annoying pet from the Faceless; there was nothing else for it. The girl and the cat would probably run, if they were smart, which would let Jin take down the Faceless without being noticed by her. That was something: if she knew someone was following her, the girl might never go to the Last Knight's hideout.

Jin took a deep breath, preparing himself to fight. He hated this kind of physical violence, as he was a genie and therefore should be using his magic to wipe these creatures from existence. But considering his lack of power, punching and kicking seemed like his only options, so he made his body more dense than normal and turned his skin as hard as steel.

If one of those swords touches you, it could do permanent damage, even to a genie, the cosmic knowledge told him.

Jin snorted. *Then I guess I'll just have to not let one touch me.*

And with that, he moved around to the side of the giant cat, ready to face the Faceless.

Only, Lena dismounted just as he did, forcing him to jump out of the way. The cat ran and hid in the trees, which made Jin even more annoyed—the animal had hunted Jin the whole time, yet ran from the *Faceless*?—but Lena didn't seem that bothered. What was she thinking, facing the creatures by herself? She might get hurt!

"What do you want with the Last Knight?" she asked,

sounding fairly calm. "He's a good friend, and I won't let you hurt him."

Jin's mouth dropped open. She was *admitting* she knew the knight? She couldn't have even *tried* to lie?

"That is not your concern," the Faceless said in unison, that creepy echoing voice making it sound like there was more than one voice in each set of armor. Someday Jin was going to need to find out exactly what the Faceless were. **"Tell us where he is or suffer the consequences."**

Lena sighed, looking sad now, of all things. "You know, this hasn't been the best day," she told the knights as they stepped forward, drawing their shadow-magic swords. "And you've been scaring my friends in the city, which puts me in an even worse mood. So." She punched one hand into the other, and the sound was like a crack of thunder, making Jin's eyes widen. "Gia—I mean, *I* fight to show you my might. *Let's do this.*"

And with that, she smiled and launched herself at the nearest Faceless.

"Tell us where—whoof!" one knight started to say, only to be interrupted by Lena's fist slamming into his stomach, sending him flying into—and then *through*—the nearest tree.

The tree splintered in half, and the top crashed to the ground, holding the Faceless in place.

Jin's mouth dropped again in surprise as the other knights all took a step back now, giving Lena a bit more room. She grinned at the fallen knight, almost a bit guiltily. "Oh, that was fun. But I didn't mean to hurt the poor tree. So if you wouldn't mind moving more to the center of the clearing, so no more trees get destroyed, I'd appreciate it."

"Taaake herrr!" the trapped Faceless growled, his voice sounding even more disjointed than usual. But there was no time to figure *that* out as the other Faceless swarmed Lena.

In spite of Lena's pretty surprising strength, Jin did not like the odds. Even someone stronger than a regular human couldn't hold out against a dozen Faceless. No, he was being left with no choice: Jin was just going to have to reveal himself and save Lena from the knights.

And once he did, he'd have to remember to teleport the Faceless somewhere far away, so they couldn't report back to the Golden King what had happened. The king was paranoid enough without finding out that his genie had fought his knights.

Jin started to turn himself visible but stopped as he realized that if he did so right in the middle of the clearing, Lena would know he'd been following her the whole time and refuse to take him to the Last Knight. He groaned, then shook his head. He'd have to pretend he just happened along in the forest.

Why was tricking people so *complicated*?

A knight went flying a few inches to his right as Jin quickly ran to the edge of the clearing, preparing himself. Another knight flew over his head, distracting him for a moment as he watched the Faceless's helmet start to come loose, only for several tiny, stringlike appendages to reach for it and *drag* it back onto the knight's body.

Uh . . . what? *That* was new. Maybe he'd have to figure out what these things were sooner rather than later.

Meanwhile, behind him, the clank of denting armor was starting to lessen, so he turned to see what was happening and gasped in surprise: There were just two knights left, and Lena wasn't even breathing hard.

"Thank you for this!" she told the knight she was facing, while the other maneuvered around behind her, his shadow-magic sword aimed at her back. She threw it a glance, but the other knight attacked, and she leapt out of the way. Together, the two Faceless might actually have a chance against her. "I really needed to punch something."

The longer Jin watched, the more he felt a weird, burning feeling in his chest, and he realized he was *angry*. Almost before he knew it, he had made himself visible and leapt straight at the second Faceless, shouting something incomprehensible, even as the creature attacked Lena with its sword.

Jin slammed into the armored monster, his dense arms and steel-like skin actually helping knock the Faceless to the ground. *"Don't touch her!"* he shouted, and the Faceless reared back in surprise, his sword just short of hitting Lena.

Jin pulled an arm back and punched the Faceless in the empty helmet, only for the visor to close over his hand, trapping him. His eyes widened, and he frantically tried to pull it out, forgetting in the heat of the moment that he could just make himself insubstantial.

But the Faceless didn't wait. Instead, it drove its sword straight at Jin and stabbed him in the shoulder.

It struck like fire, and pain went shooting through Jin's entire body, like nothing he'd ever experienced before, as he felt the sword *pulling* him, absorbing him, every second it stayed in his body. "Ahh!" he screamed, writhing on the ground as he desperately yanked the sword out and threw it away. Everything began to go dark, and he concentrated as best he could on keeping his human body together, as he couldn't reveal his genie nature, not now.

But he wasn't exactly sure he'd have a choice, as he'd never felt this *drained* before.

Someone shouted, and Jin distantly recognized that the Faceless attacking him went flying off into the woods, taking several trees with it.

"Are you okay?" said a voice, and Jin got one last look in Lena's eyes before everything faded to black, and he fell unconscious.

CHAPTER 17

Lena whirled around at the sound of someone's voice, only to scream out herself as a stranger behind her took one of the knight's swords in his shoulder.

"*NO!*" she roared, and plowed into the knight. She grabbed him by the leg and threw him across the clearing into the first knight, who was now trying to get up. The force of the hit sent them both crashing into the forest, knocking down trees as they went.

And just like that, the fight was over. Only, someone had gotten hurt, someone Lena hadn't even realized was there. Someone she could have been watching over, if she hadn't been so focused on herself.

"No no no no no," she repeated, her heart racing and guilt drowning her in waves as she quickly ran to the stranger's side.

It was a boy, one who looked like he might be around her age, but not someone she'd seen in the city before. His short brown hair looked generally familiar, but a lot of people had brown hair, and she couldn't place it. Either way, he *looked* human, but considering how much she did too, she knew that didn't prove anything.

"Are you okay?" Lena asked as she quickly reached into her pouch and pulled out the first item she could find to bandage his wound, an extra tunic. The boy didn't respond, which wasn't good. As bad as the stab had been, it shouldn't have knocked him out.

She quickly ripped her tunic in half, then wrapped it around the boy's shoulder over and over, trying not to hurt him any more than she needed to as she pulled it tight. He didn't react, which made her even more nervous.

"Hello? There's someone hurt, and I need help!" she shouted, hoping maybe there were people around to hear her, especially the Last Knight.

Too late, she realized that her shout would just lead more of the Faceless to her, if they weren't on their way already. And with the boy injured and unconscious, she couldn't stay to fight them.

The Last Knight *might* have medical supplies, but the Faceless were after him. If she went to him now, they could follow her and find him. Going back to the city wasn't any better, as she might lead the creatures there, too.

"What do I do?" she yelled, slamming her fists to the ground, sending a small tremor through the forest.

But she knew. Even Rufus knew, as he came pawing out of the woods to nuzzle her.

"Lena and I go home now?" he said quietly.

Her stomach dropped at the thought of it, but there was no choice. She nodded and carefully picked the boy up in her arms, being sure not to jostle him too much. "We're going home now," she said to her cat.

He began to purr, probably thinking that everything was okay then. "Lena is so strong!" he said, rubbing his head against her as she laid the boy stomach-first over his back. "I let you fight without me because of that."

"I know, little man," she said, and nodded down at the boy in her arms. "We need to carry him really gently, okay?"

Rufus's ears went back as he sniffed the boy. "I smelled him *before*, Lena. I smelled him before!"

Her eyebrows rose at this. "In the city?" she asked.

"Yes," Rufus said, since she'd never been able to teach him to just nod for yes.

"Then we'll have to take him back there, once he's healed," Lena said, nodding herself. Faceless or not, nothing was going to keep her from delivering this boy back to his home. He'd tried to protect her, after all, getting himself stabbed in the process! Her eyes itched just thinking about it. She didn't need the help, but *he* hadn't known that. And now look at him! All because she'd been distracted during the fight and hadn't realized he was there.

Rufus seemed to have more to say, but she just shook her head, as they didn't have any more time to waste. She climbed up behind the boy, making sure both were secure, then leaned over the boy to talk to her cat.

"Take us back home, as fast as possible," she whispered to Rufus, feeling nauseated at the very idea. But what else could she do? The boy needed help, because of *her*. She had to make sure he was okay, and there was only one way she knew to do that.

The Spark.

It healed the other giants and increased their life spans, so whatever was wrong with the boy, the Spark *had* to be able to fix it.

And the flame was also sacred to the giants, so the very thought of this human touching it would disgust them, even the ones who didn't hate humans as much as the king did. If they found out she'd used it to heal a non-giant . . . they might exile her, or *worse*.

But the boy had tried to help and gotten wounded for his trouble. No, whatever consequences there'd be, she'd accept them. But she was going to heal this boy, one way or another.

And hopefully, they just wouldn't get caught.

As Rufus kicked off with his Seven League Boots, Lena threw one last look in the direction of the Last Knight's cave. If she wasn't discovered, and was able to heal the boy, she could still make it back to the knight before nightfall. And then she could use the cauldron and return home for good.

But for now, she couldn't worry about that. The boy's injury had to come first.

The land around her blurred from the magic of Rufus's boots, focusing back up as they reappeared at the base of the mountain. He quickly lifted each paw up to her so she could take the boots off, which she did, tying them by their laces and throwing them around her neck as Rufus began to climb the mountain.

Unfortunately, even the dangerous climb couldn't distract her imagination from what might be wrong with the boy.

Maybe the sword had been magic, and now he was slowly turning into a garden slug, like poor Mr. Lettuce, who lived nearby Peter's pumpkin and every so often forgot himself and tried to eat Peter's house.

Or maybe the magic sword had somehow stolen the boy's mind, and now it was held in the Faceless's sword forever, just so the creature could have someone to talk to?

Not that it even needed to be magical. The sword could just be poisoned with something natural, meaning the boy's life was in *her* hands.

The more she considered the possibilities, the worse she felt, and the faster she wished Rufus would go.

"Hurry, my brave little man," she whispered, and the cat sped up again, even leaping so early over one of the mountain's chasms that Lena thought for sure he wouldn't make it across.

She was right. His claws scraped against the rock, finding no purchase, and they slipped down into the chasm. Lena's heart began to race so fast it almost broke through her ribs as they fell, and she had just enough time to wonder if this was it, this was how everything ended.

But at the last moment, Rufus managed to catch his claws in the dirt and pull them back up, though Lena almost slipped right off his back and into the chasm from the motion of it all.

"Okay, maybe just a little less fast," she whispered again, her heart and Rufus both slowing, at least a little bit. Somehow the boy hadn't woken up through all of that, which worried her even more.

The only good thing about that—and her nervousness about returning to her village after everything that had happened, breaking her exile—was that the trip up the mountain went by much quicker than usual, and Rufus soon was propelling them through the cloud cover and back home.

He came up so quickly, in fact, that he practically crashed into the bottom of a large leather boot.

A boot Lena recognized.

Her mother was sitting on the cloud next to the hole where the mountain jutted through. She must have been waiting for Lena to return this whole time.

Fortunately, her mother's boot blocked Lena from view, so Lena had a moment to consider all the emotions swimming around in her head. Part of her wanted to jump into her mom's arms for a hug. Part of her wanted to beg for help and apologize for leaving in the first place. And a big part of her felt sick and *angry* about how her mom and dad hadn't stood up for her, back during the ritual.

But all of that had to wait.

"I'm so sorry, Mom," Lena whispered too softly for her mother to hear as she dismounted, quickly pushed Rufus's boots onto his front paws, then jumped onto his back again.

And then they disappeared in a flash, her mother having no idea Lena had ever even returned.

Rufus reappeared on the stone walkway leading to the castle gates, and Lena swallowed hard, hating that she couldn't stop and explain things to her mother, all of it. But there was just no time.

Instead, she had returned to the last place she ever wanted to be.

The guards still stood by the gates, but now that Lena was her normal size, Rufus was able to sneak them in without being seen, ducking slightly to crawl beneath the gates. From there, he sprinted along the walls and into the castle's great hall, which was now empty, but for the Spark, which burned brightly from its spot atop the pedestal the Sparktender had stood next to during the ritual.

Lena dismounted and gently lifted the boy from Rufus's back. She thought she saw his eyes flutter for a moment but decided she must have imagined it. "Stay here with the boy," she whispered to her cat. "I'm going to bring the Spark back."

Rufus meowed slightly just as footsteps from outside the great hall shook the floor, and Lena froze in fear.

Someone was *coming*.

There was nothing for it, though. She couldn't take a chance on coming back later, not if the boy still wasn't awake. She'd have to grab the Spark and just hope she was fast enough.

If she wasn't, then at least she wouldn't have to worry about the cauldron anymore, as she and the boy would both be doomed.

CHAPTER 18

Jin woke to a burning feeling in his shoulder and an exhaustion like nothing he'd ever felt. Something was jostling him, and he opened his eyes to find himself in an unfamiliar room.

Where was he? He closed his eyes again and reached out with his magical senses, but that just confused him more. Somehow he was in a castle in the clouds . . . ?

A giant's *castle*, the cosmic knowledge said. *The girl brought you here to heal you.*

A giant's castle? Well, that was . . . something. Whatever the girl planned on doing, he wished she'd hurry, as Jin was in so much pain, he could barely keep his human body together. At least he hadn't lost control of it while unconscious, which was a pleasant surprise.

When this whole wish fulfillment thing was over, Jin decided he would *have* to find out more about the Faceless. The shadow magic in their weapons was *dangerous*. He'd almost died just from one stab! If the Golden King had the power to actually do away with Jin, he might decide to use it, if he were angry enough.

Jin gently reached out with his senses toward his shoulder, hoping to gain more information from the injury, only to find something odd: it wasn't just that the sword had cut him, but part of his power was . . . *gone*. Completely removed somehow, as if the sword had cut away the magical part of him, leaving him weak and in incredible pain.

Am I going to heal? Get my magic back? he asked the cosmic knowledge, a cold, sinking feeling in his stomach.

It went silent for a moment, and Jin found himself holding his breath. *No,* it said finally. *Not without some sort of influx of magic, you won't. At this point, you have just enough magic to control your own body. But even teleporting is out.*

Which meant not only was he stuck in the cloud city of giants, but he had no way of getting home, with or without the Last Knight. Jin sighed. *Well, at least I'm humbled! That should count for something, right? And get me out of my service to the king?*

It might if you were humbled, but trust me, you're not.

Jin swore. *This is why no one likes you, you know.*

See, now you're just projecting.

The jostling stopped, and Jin quickly closed his eyes again as someone lifted him up, then gently set him down on the cold stone floor. After a moment of silence, he cracked one eye and almost shrieked in surprise as he found the cat's giant head just inches from his face.

"Stay here with the boy," Lena said to the cat as he licked his lips. "I'm going to bring the Spark back."

Rufus meowed, his look showing zero mercy as he moved in. Right before Jin could object and call the girl back, the floor trembled from booming footsteps that sounded as if they were coming this way.

"Get off me," Jin said, pushing the cat's giant mouth away from him. He tried to push to his feet, only for his shoulder to start screaming in agony when he put pressure on it. The surprise pain sent him crashing to the floor, landing hard on his back.

"Lena!" the cat hissed, and from across the room the girl looked back, which was embarrassing. Why couldn't the girl's spell that made him so nervous around her be the part that the shadow magic had stolen?

Because that spell doesn't exist, and you just have a crush?

"Don't move!" Lena hissed from the bottom of an enormous pedestal. "I've got something that will heal you right up!" She glanced up at it, then leapt into the air, going far higher than any human could jump, which Jin would have found odd if the pain in his shoulder hadn't been so distracting. At the top of her jump, she threw her arms around the pedestal, somehow grabbed ahold of it, then began climbing quickly to the top.

It was hard to tell from the distance, but it almost looked like she was digging handholds in the marble pedestal using just her fingers. But again, that couldn't be possible.

The footsteps shook the room again, closer this time. Jin winced and tried to stand once more, only for the cat to lay a paw on his chest and push him back down.

"Lena says stay," the cat told him, licking his lips again. Fantastic. And Jin couldn't do anything about it, because he was too weak.

This day was *not* going how he'd planned. Not even a little bit.

"Okay, I'll stay," he told the monster, holding up his hands in surrender. *But if you try to eat me,* Jin thought, *I hope I have enough magic left to transform into something poisonous.*

You don't.

Lena's climb didn't take long, but it did give Jin some time to examine his surroundings, which was a lot more useful than watching the cat eye him hungrily. It looked as if they were in an enormous hall of the castle, though the word "enormous" didn't do the room justice. Most of the Golden King's castle could have easily fit in just this one room.

Which meant the footsteps were either a guard or the owner of the castle, neither of which Jin found particularly comforting, especially given his condition and the lack of teleporting. What was he going to do if a giant showed up? Faceless were one thing, but he doubted even Lena could handle a giant.

But she *did* seem familiar with the place, or at least whatever she was climbing to get. Was the girl working with the giants? Stealing from them? This added new uncertainty to a plan that already was filled with it.

Maybe he could get some information while he waited, at least. "Is Lena a friend of the giants?" he asked the cat, having no idea what else to do.

"Lena *is* a giant," the cat said, and Jin rolled his eyes. Well, that was pointless: clearly the animal had no idea what it was talking about and therefore was useless. Fortunately, the girl waved from the top of the column now and looked like she had something in her hands, a dish of some kind, around the size of a serving bowl. All she'd need to do was climb down. . . .

Except instead of doing the safe, normal thing, the girl just leapt straight off the top.

"No!" Jin shouted, pushing the cat aside to try to do something, but it was way too late to stop her, and he had nowhere near enough magic to catch her. Instead, he watched helplessly as she came crashing to the floor, hitting much more quietly than the approaching giant's footsteps, but still hard enough to break every bone in her body.

And then, in what was just another incomprehensible part of the day, the girl shook it off, then sprinted over to them, holding a bowl of fire in her hands like nothing impossible had just happened.

"What . . . *how?*" Jin sputtered as she neared.

"Oh, that?" she said, sounding sincerely like she hadn't given it a thought. "Don't worry, I'm stronger than I look."

That he knew, after the fight against the Faceless. But still, what kind of human could do things like this?

And why do you care so much? Because of her "magic spell," right? You be quiet.

"We don't have much time," she said, carefully setting the

bowl of fire down next to Jin. "We have to get out of here before the king arrives, or . . . well, bad things."

Jin raised an eyebrow at what those bad things might be, but he was more curious about the flame. Oddly, the fire didn't give off heat, like he'd expect. And weirdly, it almost felt . . . familiar, filled with a kind of magic that Jin recognized somehow.

What is this stuff? he asked the cosmic knowledge.

It paused for a moment. *Jin, be careful,* it said finally, a note of worry he'd rarely heard in its voice. *There's something about that flame. . . .*

But Lena helped him to a sitting position before he could respond. "I know this sounds odd, but let me touch the Spark to your shoulder. It can heal you." She paused, like she wanted to add, *I hope.* Or maybe that was just Jin thinking it.

"Won't it burn me?" Jin asked, both trying to pretend to be a normal human and honestly not sure what this fire was. The little the cosmic knowledge had said didn't exactly fill him with confidence.

She shook her head. "It'll all be okay. Watch." She took a deep breath, then pushed her own hand into the flame without even flinching. She stared at her hand in the fire for a moment, her face unreadable to Jin, before pulling her hand back out, unburned. "See?" she said, her voice now full of emotion. "Won't hurt at all."

He nodded, wondering what had just happened, as well as still not entirely convinced as she slowly helped him closer to the flame. He leaned over, wincing from the pain, and she guided his shoulder toward the flame, or the Spark, whatever she'd called it.

Well, this was going to be interesting, either way.

Wait! the cosmic knowledge said. *Don't touch it. I don't know what—*

And then Lena pushed the fire into his shoulder. "Please, make him *whole* again," she whispered, just as the flame touched his skin.

Every molecule in Jin's body instantly exploded with magical power, and his mind opened like never before. He tried to speak, or even to think, but the power was too intense. It was like being blasted with hurricane winds and trying to keep your footing.

From what felt like miles away, he felt the floor drop away from his feet, like he was flying, and part of him knew that shouldn't be happening, but the rest of him was too enraptured by the magic to care.

"What?" shouted a voice loud enough to shake the floor below Jin, though he felt like he only heard it from a great distance. "What is going *on* here?"

"It's the *king*!" he heard Lena hiss from miles away. "We need to run, *now*!"

CHAPTER 19

Touching the Spark had been bad enough for Lena. As she'd put her hand into its flame, all she could think about was how she hadn't been allowed to do this at the ritual, in front of her family and the other giants. She hadn't been allowed to be given a *name* by the Sparktender.

She hadn't been allowed to be declared a true giant.

But then the Spark had made the boy float and explode with light, something she'd never heard of happening before. And before she could even tell if he was okay, King Denir, the last giant she ever wanted to see again, entered the room and saw everything.

There was no going back from this. All her dreams of living in the giant village, being accepted at her true size, having her own epithet . . . those were all gone now. She knew this, even as she knew she couldn't afford to feel any of that at the moment, not while the king could still catch them.

"It's the *king*!" she hissed at the boy, hoping he could hear in spite of him still glowing brightly. "We need to run, *now*!"

He didn't respond, but his light was getting brighter. She quickly pulled the Spark away from him, hoping that would help, and it seemed to, as the boy slowly floated back to the floor and collapsed in a heap.

"YOU!" King Denir roared, clenching his enormous hands into fists. "You *dare* touch the Spark, you monster?" And then his gaze fell upon the boy, and if anything, he grew even more enraged. "A human? *You let* a human *touch the sacred flame?*"

Trying desperately not to think about what was coming, Lena picked the boy up and threw him on Rufus's back. The king seemed to figure out that she meant to run and slammed the doors to the great hall shut behind him, then grabbed a spear from the wall next to the doors and aimed it directly at Lena.

"Rufus, take him to Treats Lady!" she shouted, and gave her cat a push. But as he looked back at her in confusion and fear, the king slammed his foot down on the floor, sending a shock wave straight at them.

It hit before either Lena or Rufus could move out of its way, throwing them into the air. Rufus meowed in fright, his feet scrambling uselessly, while Lena grabbed for the Spark, desperate to make sure the bowl didn't break if it hit the floor.

The group crashed down a moment later as the king ran to them, his footsteps shaking the floor enough to make it hard to even keep their feet. But they had no choice: there was only one way out of the great hall, and that was right through the doors on the other side of the king.

"I knew you were secretly one of them!" he roared as he neared, almost close enough to stab them with his spear. "You always meant to steal the Spark, didn't you? *Betrayer!*"

Two guards entered the room behind the king and shut the doors again, blocking the open space beneath the doors with their feet as best they could. Lena wanted to scream, cry, or both, having no idea what to do. Even Rufus with his boots was stuck now, and there was no other exit, or even a place to hide.

And then she looked down at the Spark in her hand.

"You will *pay* for defiling the Spark with your touch!" the king roared, aiming his spear. The enormous blade would be too large to dodge, and Lena knew her tiny little compass arrow would have no effect on something so big and with so much force behind it.

Not knowing what else to do, she hugged Rufus tightly, the

Spark's flame touching her hand as she tried to keep ahold of it. "It's going to be okay, little man," she whispered to him, feeling him shaking beneath her. "It's all going to be okay."

"Thieves!" the king shouted, and stabbed at them with the spear.

Lena scrunched her eyes closed, and without any other options, prayed to anyone who was listening.

Please, she thought, *at least let the boy get home safely. He doesn't deserve any of this.*

And then she waited for the spear to hit.

But it never did. Instead, she heard the king roar "NO—" before being cut off suddenly. And then just as abruptly, there were voices all around them, quieter voices, sounding more surprised than anything.

Lena opened one eye, then the other, gasping at what she saw before her.

They were no longer in the giant king's great hall, nor in his castle, the giant village, or even probably in the clouds.

Instead, they were surrounded by people in very fancy clothes, all accented with silver and bronze, eating what looked like a great feast. Lena looked down and found that she and Rufus were standing on a table a dozen yards long, filled with foods of all kinds.

But weirdest of all, everything besides the fancy clothes people wore was made of gold, from the napkins on the table to the drapes over the windows, from the rugs on the floor to the crown on the very angry-looking man at the head of the table.

"*More* rebels?" the man in the crown, a *king*, shouted, leaping to his feet. He reached for Lena with a hand wearing a golden glove, looking like he meant to threaten her, though she didn't understand how.

"We're not rebels!" Lena shouted quickly, throwing up her hands in surrender. "We were . . . we, uh . . . we were running for our lives, and something brought us here, I guess? I'm not entirely sure how, honestly."

"The boy is gone," Rufus pointed out, which sent a wave of terror down Lena's spine. She looked over to see what he meant and discovered that yes, the boy *was* gone, completely disappeared from where he'd been lying on her cat's back.

Had she left him behind in the great hall? But no, she couldn't have, not if Rufus was here too . . . could she?

"A boy?" the king said, his glove still aimed in her direction, which seemed odd. What was he planning on doing with it? "*What* boy?"

"I don't know his name," Lena said, shaking her head. "But

he helped me against the Faceless, and was wounded, so I just . . . I wanted him to get home safely."

"The Faceless?" one of the diners whispered, and winced as Lena glanced at her. "Uh-oh."

The king frowned at this, looking her and her cat over. "This boy . . . what did he look like?"

"Brown hair, brown eyes, fairly ordinary," Lena said quickly, just glad the man seemed less angry and wasn't going to glove them, at least not at the moment. But even as she described the boy, she wondered why that was all she'd noticed. It was almost as if the boy's appearance was designed to be forgettable. "A bit cranky-looking, if that makes sense?"

The man glanced down at his non-gloved hand, where he wore a large ring. He paused for a moment, then his gaze went to the floor. "And that?" he asked, pointing down at her hand.

Lena followed his finger, only for her heart to stop as she saw what he was asking about. "That . . . is the Spark," she said in horror, as the giants' most precious treasure burned away in its bowl in her grasp, the treasure that she'd just *stolen*, in spite of all her denials that she was doing just that. "And I'm in very, *very* big trouble."

CHAPTER 20

agic was *everywhere*. He could see it, feel it, manipulate it. Anything he wanted to do, he could, from the smallest of spells to the ultimate creation or destruction of entire universes.

Part of him was terrified by it all. At the slightest twitch of his pinkie, he could flick an entire city out of existence. Or if he blinked, he might accidentally change it so that the land had tides, and the sea stood still. He might breathe out and unleash hurricanes across the world, or sigh and create a sadness that overwhelmed every living thing, making it feel useless to even go on.

But the other part of Jin knew that *this* was who he was. This was the power of a genie unleashed, an ifrit. And someday it would be his.

SOMEDAY? said a voice from somewhere around him. It sounded a bit like the cosmic knowledge, but different enough that he knew they weren't the same. *WHY NOT TODAY?*

A rush of power flowed through Jin, and he found it hard to remember why he was afraid. Any mistake he made, he could just *un*make. There were no limits to what he could do!

"How?" he asked, not sure where the voice was coming from. "I'm still bound to the Golden King. I have more wishes to fulfill. And even after that, the elder genies want me to show humility."

HUMILITY? GENIES ARE ALL-POWERFUL. WHY WOULD YOU NEED TO BE HUMBLE?

"Right?" Jin said, feeling another rush just that someone finally agreed with him. "I never did understand the point of that!"

YOU'VE BEEN HELD BACK FOR TOO LONG, JIN, the voice said, and now he could sense its location: it was coming from the magic inside him, all around him. It was the magic itself!

Hey, cosmic knowledge, Jin thought. *Are you seeing this? The magic is talking to me! It says I deserve to have my power back. What do you say to* that?

But there was no response from the cosmic knowledge, and he wondered if it was being blocked somehow by all the power he now felt. Who needed it, though, if he could do whatever he wanted, find out anything he needed to know?

YOU CAN DO ALL THAT AND MORE, the voice said. *THE SCRAPS OF KNOWLEDGE ALLOWED YOU ARE ONLY THERE TO CONFUSE YOU, TO HOLD YOU BACK. THEY DON'T WANT YOU GAINING YOUR RIGHTFUL POWER, THREATENING THEIR CONTROL.*

He'd never really considered it that way. Why did they want to hold back all the knowledge of the universe from him, if not to control him in some way? What could be wrong with knowing everything?

EMBRACE ME, the voice said. *FREE ME FROM THIS FIRE, THIS* SPARK, *AND YOU WILL HAVE ALL THE POWER YOU WERE ALWAYS MEANT TO, THE POWER THAT YOU SHOULD HAVE HAD FROM THE START.*

Jin's eyes lit up. "Permanently? I can go back to my home dimension and leave this horrible human world for good?"

YOU'LL BE ABLE TO DO WHATEVER YOU WANT. IF YOU WISHED IT, YOU COULD SHAPE THIS *WORLD INTO YOUR IDEAL HOME. MAKE THE HUMANS FULFILL* YOUR *WISHES.*

Jin laughed. "Now *that's* an interesting idea. I'd love to see the Golden King waiting on *my* wishes for a change." But as he said this, the magic around him began to disappear. "Wait, where are you going? Come back!"

YOU ARE NO LONGER IN CONTACT WITH MY SPARK. YOU MUST TAKE IT BACK AND FREE ME IF YOU WISH TO HAVE THE MAGIC YOU'RE OWED. FIND ME, FREE ME, YOUNG GENIE.

"Not in contact with your Spark?" Jin said, confused. "But what happened? Where did it go? I thought Lena . . ." He trailed off as an image of the girl filled his head, trying to heal him with the power of the Spark, all because she thought he had been trying to protect her.

THE GIRL IS OF NO IMPORTANCE. NO HUMAN OR GIANT IS. THEY ARE ANTS BENEATH THE FEET OF THE TRULY POWERFUL, LIKE YOU.

Jin couldn't really deny *that*. Humans and giants both seemed equally annoying, and having to serve someone like the Golden King really was the worst. But still, Lena seemed different somehow. . . .

FIND ME, AND THE POWER YOU DESERVE SHALL BE YOURS, the voice said one last time before disappearing along with the rest of the magic.

As the voice faded, so did Jin's energy, leaving him sapped and tired, though not anywhere close to as bad as he felt after getting stabbed by the shadow-magic sword. Still, doubts began to form, and he wondered exactly what the Spark really was as the world around him came back into view, looking far more purple than he'd expected. But he was too tired to worry about that at the moment.

A few minutes of resting on something soft and comfortable helped quite a bit, and Jin's energy slowly began to return. As it did, he looked around, realizing he was no longer in the giant's castle and instead was somewhere far more familiar: his ring, the one that the Golden King used to control him.

Inside the jewel were luxurious, well-furnished chambers, which was good, because Jin had spent years inside here already. It had been lonely at times, but at least he hadn't had to listen to wishes from selfish humans.

He let himself relax on one of the purple sofas and let out a huge sigh, content not to think about any of this until the Golden King called him again. All the pain from being stabbed had somehow disappeared, healed along with the wound itself, which meant he could just lie back and rest.

As he closed his eyes, something irritating flitted around his mind, something he couldn't quite remember. He opened one eye, just to look around. Everything looked normal, here in the ring, so it wasn't that.

What had he been doing before the Spark, though? He cast his memory back and seemed to recall there was something important, something he wasn't doing.

You were fulfilling a wish, the cosmic knowledge said in his head.

The wish! Jin sat up too quickly, and his head began to pound. *Ow. And hey, where did you go? I had questions about something, and you were gone. I could feel it.*

Questions about what? The cosmic knowledge sounded confused, of all things. *That* shouldn't have been possible. *What do you mean?*

It . . . doesn't matter, Jin said, finding himself not wanting to discuss it for some reason. The Spark had left him with too many questions, and he wasn't sure he wanted to know the answers.

But how had he gotten back to the ring? Had the Golden King recalled him for some reason? And Lena would have . . .

Wait, where was *Lena*?

"What happened?" Jin shouted, leaping to his feet. "How

did I get back here? Last I remember, Lena was healing me with that flame. Where *is* she?"

I can tell you, but you may not like the answer. Do you really want to know?

"Of course I want to know!" Jin shouted.

Why? Because of the "magic spell" she put on you? The knowledge seemed to think it was being funny.

"Because she was my lead to the Last Knight!" Jin shouted, thankful to have a reason, instead of the gnawing uncomfortable emptiness in the pit of his stomach at the moment. That emptiness had to be the remains of her spell . . . right? "Without her, I may never find him. Now tell me where she is! How did I get back here?"

At the moment, the Golden King has her.

Jin wasn't presently in human form, so he didn't actually have any blood, but if he had, it would have run cold in his veins. *"What?"*

I told you that you might not like the answer.

"But how? We were nowhere near his castle. He could have called me back, but *she* would have stayed . . . wherever we were."

The flame she used to heal you was made of pure magic. She accidentally used its power to bring you home and was taken along with you.

Jin immediately flew straight to the top of the ring, banging his hands against it. "Your Majesty!" he shouted, not even sure if the king could hear him. "Let me out! I need to speak to you!"

But no one answered, and Jin remained unsummoned.

He floated back down to his luxurious couch, suddenly not at all comforted by it. What could be happening outside now? Had the king thrown the girl in the dungeon, or worse? Could he be torturing her for information about the Last Knight?

The possibilities were endless, and if Jin didn't get out soon, he was going to explode with worry.

CHAPTER 21

'm sorry—if I eat any more, I might explode," Lena said to one of the king's servants in a side room, waving away the offer of more food. "It's all very delicious, thank you. But I really need to speak to the king again. I need to find the boy I came here with, and make sure he's all right." She paused, dreading asking the next question, but needing it to sound casual, so they wouldn't notice she was terrified. "Oh, and the flame I arrived with is really important, so I'd like to have it back, if that's okay."

The man who brought her food smiled slightly, his clothes made from gold, just like the king's had been. "I'm sorry, miss, but the king is very busy. He will summon you when he is free, I'm sure."

And with that, he left her alone in the room and, just like

every time he'd exited, locked the door behind him.

She dropped her head into her hands and groaned as Rufus made loud chomping noises from the table next to her, getting the stew he was eating everywhere.

Here she was, locked away in the Golden King's castle. All she knew about him came from Mrs. Hubbard and the others in the Cursed City, but none of the stories were good. In fact, he sounded like a horrible tyrant who wanted to destroy the city and the Last Knight.

And now he had the Spark. Not only had Lena accidentally stolen the giants' most sacred object, but she'd handed it over to the Cursed City's worst enemy.

Not to mention that no one would tell her if the boy was here, or if he was okay!

"Food is good," Rufus said, not looking up from his bowl, his third helping.

She petted his head, trying to avoid the various splashes of stew in his fur. "I couldn't actually eat much," she said, pushing the plate in front of her away. She'd lied and said she'd had enough, but in reality, she felt too sick to eat and just wanted the servant to take her to the king.

Instead, she was locked in some side chamber, just as golden as the main dining room she'd landed in earlier, and had no idea what to do.

Trying to keep from despairing about it all, she decided to work out how exactly she'd gotten here. It had to be the Spark, of course. It clearly did more than just healing. Somehow it'd heard her thoughts and brought them all to the Golden King's castle, trading one horrible king for another.

But she'd asked for the boy to get home safely. And if this *was* the boy's home, that brought up all kinds of questions, like how he'd been in the clearing to help her against the Faceless, and how he knew about the Cursed City.

Not to mention that he lived with the Golden King, the leader of the Faceless. So why help her?

Part of her wanted to take Rufus and just run, get away. But if she did that now, she'd be leaving both the boy *and* the Spark behind, since the king had taken it from her hands before she knew what was happening. Fortunately, and surprisingly, the king had acted oddly decent to her, at least so far. In spite of the fact that she'd appeared out of nowhere in his dining room, practically landing right on his chair with him, he hadn't had her thrown in the dungeon or anything.

Instead, he had his servants take care of her, feeding her and giving her a place to stay while he finished with his feast in the main dining room. He *had* taken the Spark, yes, but he claimed it was just so he could make sure it wasn't dangerous, as he didn't know who she was any better than Lena knew him. It was hard to argue with that.

But no matter what the king had said, she wasn't going to be able to sit here for much longer. As it was, she had to keep telling herself to stay calm and wait, that she was a stranger here, and she had to be polite and patient.

The only problem was, patience was overrated. Punching holes in walls and leaving, meanwhile, was much more satisfying.

"Okay, calm down," she told herself, unclenching her fists and dropping her palms onto the table. "You need to relax. Take deep breaths." She closed her eyes and did just that, only opening them as she felt something odd beneath her palms. She looked down and discovered that she'd left handprints in the surface of the golden table, which didn't seem like the best way to get in the king's good graces.

"Lena is angry?" Rufus asked, stew dripping from his mouth as he looked up at her curiously.

"Lena is scared, little man," she said. "Not for us, but for that boy."

Rufus's ears went back. "The boy hunted us. He was in Treats Lady's den."

She frowned at this. "What do you mean? In the Boot-ique? I didn't see him there."

Before her cat could respond, the door opened, and the Golden King strode in, smiling widely, the Spark in his hand. Just the sight of it made Lena feel a *bit* less anxious, though she'd have felt a lot better if *she* were the one holding it.

"I hope you've had a good meal, my young friend," the king said to her as she quickly stood up and bowed, hoping that was the right move. He waved her to sit back down and took a seat across from her and Rufus. "Was everything to your liking?"

"Oh, yes, of course, it was great, Your, ah, Majesty," Lena said, stumbling over her words a bit. The giant king's protocol she knew, but human royalty was a new concept to her, and she wasn't sure how they liked to be treated. "I'm worried about the boy I came with, though. No one can tell me if he's okay, or even if he's here."

The king nodded. "Yes, the boy. He's, ah, just fine." He absently tapped a gloved hand against the table, and it made a metallic noise, like he was wearing a ring beneath it. He looked away for a moment before turning back to Lena. "You have my word on that. Don't you worry a bit."

Lena let out a huge sigh of relief, collapsing back into her chair. "That's . . . that's *great* news," she said, smiling slightly. "I honestly was worried!"

"Where exactly did you meet him, if you don't mind my asking?" the king said, frowning slightly.

"Oh, in the woods, outside of . . . my village," Lena said, cringing inside at the lie. She couldn't let the king know she'd come from the Cursed City, or that the king's own soldiers had been attacking her and the boy, though. The Faceless had been searching for the Last Knight, most likely on the king's orders, so she had to keep all of that quiet, or else he might start questioning her about the knight, too. "But if you say he's okay, then that's all I need to know. Can I see him?"

The king's frown deepened. "Oh, I'm afraid not. He's one of my *personal* servants and has been given an extremely important task to fulfill." He looked up at Lena with one eyebrow raised. "He didn't mention anything about it, did he?"

"No, I didn't even get his name," Lena said, feeling a strange sense of sadness over not getting to apologize to the boy and thank him for trying to help her against the Faceless. Even if he did work for their leader. "Please tell him I really appreciate everything he did for me, though."

The king nodded. "I will. Now tell me about yourself. You seem . . . tall for a child, yet you mentioned to one of my servants that you are only twelve. You *are* fully human, aren't you?"

Part of her wanted to just admit the truth about being a giant, especially knowing that if she kept lying now, it would only cascade until she lost control of it altogether. But as nice as this king was acting, she knew she couldn't trust him, not after everything she'd heard in the Cursed City. "Just . . . tall for my age, I guess," she said, inwardly sighing at how far from reality that statement was.

He stared at her for a moment, making her wonder if he could tell she was lying, but then turned to the Spark in his hands. "And this? My advisors tell me that it isn't going to burn down my castle, which I'm thankful for." He laughed like he'd made a joke, and Lena joined him, trying to be polite.

"That's the Spark," she said, reaching closer to take it. The king, however, didn't pass it over, so she pulled her hand back awkwardly. "It's, uh, a family heirloom."

"And what does it do?" He smiled. "Again, if you don't mind my asking."

"Of course not," Lena said, her mind racing about what to say, considering she'd already lied about being a giant. Given that, how could she explain the Spark? "It's mostly just been used for . . . healing."

Both the king's eyebrows rose now. "Healing? This flame? How does it work?"

Now he placed it in the middle of the table, just close enough for Lena to reach the fire, but too far away to look like he was handing it over. She took a deep breath, then stuck a hand into the flame, waving it around to show she wasn't burned. "See?" she said, her voice cracking at having to touch the Spark again. "Very safe. But if you don't mind, I really should get it back to my family—"

"Healing," the king said again, pulling the Spark back over to his side. "Interesting. How powerful is it? Could it heal some sort of . . . magical curse, do you think?"

"Oh, maybe?" Lena said, wondering if the king needed a curse broken. If she could help him with it, he might return the Spark in thanks. Maybe he'd even be willing to call his Faceless back from the Cursed City, if he really needed the help? "Did you have someone cursed who needs healing?"

The king smiled slowly. "You know, I often tell the story

about how my father, the king, decided to test his children, and see which was his most worthy heir. We all went out and brought him back an object that most symbolized power to each of us, and it went like you might expect." He leaned closer, staring at Lena. "But the part I usually leave out is that the winner was actually my youngest sister. We boys all left on adventures and brought back shadow magic and genies, but *she* just walked down to my father's library and brought back a pile of books."

"Books?" Lena asked, not sure what any of this meant.

"She was claiming knowledge and wisdom were the ultimate power," the king said, waving his golden-gloved hand absently. "And my father declared her the winner. Unfortunately, I wasn't too happy about that, so I used the glove I found to turn him and my brothers to gold."

Lena's eyes widened, and she slowly looked down at the golden glove on his hand.

The king glanced away for a moment. "She was never in any danger, of course, both because she's always been my favorite, and because she was wise enough not to be around when we returned. I think about her often, wondering how she's doing."

Then the king reached out and touched his golden glove to

Rufus's head. Before Rufus could move, a wave of gold swept down over him, turning his fur and skin to gold, freezing him in place as a statue.

It all happened too quickly for Lena to even react. As she slowly stood up, her heart racing as her entire body went cold, she couldn't breathe, couldn't speak. "What . . . what did you *do*?" she whispered, not able to believe it.

"Oh, I turned your enormous cat to gold," the king said, holding the Spark in his hand. "Now, I suggest you explain to me how this fire works, so I can try it on your cat. Like my sister said, knowledge is power, child. So either give me that knowledge, or your pet stays golden *forever*."

CHAPTER 22

Jin paced around in his luxurious other-dimensional home, muttering to himself. The comfortable couch was now lying on its side after he tried using it to break out of the ring, hoping it might open a way for him to escape. He might have known that'd be impossible, if his cosmic knowledge wasn't being so *useless*.

I heard that, you know.

Good! Jin thought back. *You were meant to! I hope you're offended enough to* do *something and help me get out of here!*

There is no way out. The ring is your prison until such time as you've learned humility and committed a selfless act. Either that, or after one thousand and thirty-eight more years of service, which seems like it'll happen sooner.

Jin growled, pulling at the hair he'd added to his head just to pull on. "Okay!" he shouted out loud. "I hereby am going to commit a selfless act by saving Lena. See? Now let me out!"

Nice try.

Jin screamed out a few thoughts of his own, specifically about where the cosmic knowledge might go.

Well, now I wouldn't help you even if you were being selfless! That was just rude, not to mention impossible, even for me.

Jin growled in frustration and slid down the nearest wall, dropping his head into his hands. What was going *on* outside? Why hadn't the Golden King summoned him yet? He had to know Jin had returned, and there was no Last Knight in sight.

So why wasn't the Golden King punishing him for failing, or at least demanding an answer?

The only possibility was that the king was distracted by Lena, and maybe the Spark, if she still had it on her. And if she did, then the king would most likely be torturing her to figure out how it worked.

The thought of Lena in pain made Jin want to throw up, something he wasn't even sure he could do in his spirit form, inside the ring.

Honestly, even I am a little surprised by how much you've taken to this girl. I mean, I knew it was coming, and what choices you'd make because of it, but still. Look at you. You're so upset about an earthly creature!

"No, I'm *not*," Jin said, rolling his eyes. "She clearly used a spell on me! And besides, she's my only link to the Last Knight. That's it! I'm just here to finish my wishes so I can get away from the Golden King, okay?"

Mm-hm.

The cosmic knowledge was *not* helping, so Jin tuned him out, trying to stay calm.

Five minutes later he tried throwing the couch against the ceiling again. This time, it split apart when it crashed back to the floor.

Satisfied?

"No!" Jin shouted. "All I want to do is *get out there and—*"

Midway through his yell he found himself staring at the Golden King, in the middle of an otherwise empty throne room. The king raised an eyebrow at Jin's words.

"Get out there and what, *genie?*" he asked.

"Get out there and make your wish come true," Jin finished quickly, bowing low. "I'm truly sorry I haven't yet found the Last Knight, Your Majesty. But I know *how* to find him, and—"

The Golden King put a hand up to stop him. "That can wait."

Jin's eyes widened in shock. It could *what*? There was nothing that made the king angrier than the rebels, and the Last Knight was the most rebel-y of all. And that was before the knight had humiliated the king in his throne room, too. "I must have misheard you, Your Majesty, as I thought you said—"

"Oh, I'll be punishing you for your failure, of course," the king said, and Jin felt his throat tighten in anticipation. "And the Last Knight's capture remains a top priority. But for now, I need to know everything about the girl you brought here."

A million different emotions exploded in Jin's head at once. What had the king done to Lena? Had he hurt her? Was he holding her hostage? What was going on?

But he couldn't let the king know he cared at all, or he'd make it all so much worse for *both* of them. "A girl, you say? I'm not sure who you're talking about."

The king smiled and beckoned someone to come in from the side of the room.

Jin slowly turned to find several Faceless knights carrying two golden statues into the throne room. One was a large cat, *Lena's* cat, and the other—

Jin's mouth dropped open in horror as he stared at a perfectly rendered statue of Lena in gold.

"You should see what she did to my antechamber," the king said as Jin discovered he was having a hard time breathing, now that he was back in human form. "She refused my simple request, then took down half a squad of Faceless before I decided enough was enough and turned her to gold."

"Is she . . . ," Jin started to say, but felt his mouth go dry, something that had never happened to him before, and he couldn't get the words out.

"Alive?" the king said. "Of course, just like all the rest." He pointed at the other statues lining the room, including those of the various rebels he'd captured over the years. "All I asked her to do was explain to me how to use the magical Spark she had to restore her cat back from a golden statue, and she just went wild, attacking all the guards, even *me*!" He seemed more offended by this than anything. "So tell me, *who* is this girl, and why did you bring her here?"

"She's . . . no one," Jin said, staring at her golden eyes, frozen now in anger. Even her fists were still raised and ready to fight, like she was a moment away from punching whoever dared stand between her and her pet. "Just some girl I met along the way. Some of your Faceless attacked me, not knowing I worked for you, and one stabbed me." He turned back to the king, using the anger he felt over that prior pain to push past his other feelings. "What kind of swords do they have, anyway? It really hurt!"

"That's none of your concern," the king said, smiling slightly. "Though it's good to know that even *you* are vulnerable to them. Even if you fail me in other ways, we'll still have that to fall back on."

Jin blinked, his emotions swirling around in his head, making it hard to concentrate on anything. If he failed, they'd have *what* to fall back on? The Faceless's swords? What did that mean?

"Still, that doesn't answer my question. She has some kind of abnormal strength, and that cat has obviously been magically modified. So again, I *order* you to tell me who this girl is, this enchanted creature who you *brought into my dining room without warning and who could have killed me* . . . or your punishment for failure will be *doubled*."

Ah, so that was what the king was so angry about. Jin swallowed hard. "I . . . honestly don't know. All I got was her name. I don't even know where she took me to heal me." That was mostly the truth, with just a few facts left out here and there. Still, he figured the Golden King would buy it.

The king narrowed his eyes, then held up the Spark. "And this?"

Uh-oh. The king having the Spark was *definitely* not good. But if Jin explained what it was—or at least the little he knew about it, since he still wasn't sure he really understood what it was—there was no way the king would ever part with it.

"I know as much as you do," Jin lied, shrugging. "It's called the Spark, and it was able to heal me, but beyond that, I have no idea. Probably just an old enchanted item, not worth anything."

"Oh, it's much more than that," the king said quietly, making Jin inwardly wince. "It's confounding my advisors, but from what they can tell me, this fire is *pure magic*. Its possibilities are endless, if one knows how to access its power." The Spark reflected in his eyes, making them burn. "Just think, genie. I could do *anything* I wanted. Snap my fingers and bring the Last Knight to me here, instantly, without relying on your pathetic help. Or burn all the remaining rebels where they stand. No one could stand against me, not even one of your power!"

Jin took a step back anxiously and put his hands up to slow things down. "I don't know if it could do all that. . . ."

The king grinned in a way that made Jin extremely

uncomfortable. "Oh, it can. And now we'll see together." He held the Spark out toward Jin, and he felt a strange buzz pass through him at the memory of its power. "I gave the girl a chance to save her pet. All she had to do was show me how to use it, but she refused. I'll make you the same deal. Show me what this is, and how to use it . . . and I'll let the girl go. Otherwise, I have a couple of new statues for my throne room. What do you say, genie?"

CHAPTER 23

The Golden King had only touched Lena with his glove, but whatever he'd done had sent her somewhere . . . *else*. She could still think, sort of, but couldn't move an inch. And thinking was getting harder with every moment that passed, like she was struggling to stay awake. It didn't help that everything around her was silent and dark in whatever prison he'd stuck her in.

Part of her wondered if he'd also turned her to gold, like he'd done to Rufus, but remembering her poor cat's fate just enraged her, making her feel even more powerless that she couldn't help him.

She should have run the moment she saw the king, back in his dining room. Just grabbed the Spark and had it take her and Rufus somewhere, *anywhere* else. The boy, too . . .

Except no, the boy worked for the king. And that meant that whoever he was, he was probably some kind of spy, maybe even looking for the Last Knight. That'd explain what he was doing in the forest outside the Cursed City . . . but not why the Faceless attacked him.

None of it made any sense, and that just added to her frustration. She tried to scream, release some of her pent-up rage, but found that impossible too, which made her feel even angrier.

None of this would have happened if she hadn't insisted on going to the ritual with her parents. Couldn't she have just kept hiding out in her cottage, avoiding the other villagers? Then Rufus would be okay, and she wouldn't have maybe led a spy toward the Last Knight. If she could have just put up with wearing the Growth Ring when needed, pretending to be someone she wasn't . . . never being acknowledged as a giant with the rest of the kids . . .

No. As much as it might have fixed things, she just couldn't take that life for much longer. She just *couldn't*, not after spending so many years of her life hiding, waiting to turn twelve and to start to become a true giant in the eyes of the village, and get her real name.

Yes, everything had gone horribly, and she desperately

missed her parents, the giant village, even some of the giants themselves. But if she could figure some way out of her current imprisonment and rescue Rufus, she might still be able to find the Last Knight, use the cauldron, and . . .

And what? Go back to her village? King Denir would never allow it, not even if she returned the Spark. If he didn't stab her with his spear the moment she returned, she could at best hope for exile, and to live out the rest of her life in the Cursed City. And that wasn't even the most likely possibility.

No, at this point she might as well resign herself to living with the humans and hope to return the Spark some way without the giant king catching her. Which meant she'd have to keep hiding her true self from the Cursed City residents, so that they wouldn't start fearing her too.

And if that was her life, was it any better than hiding her true self back in the giant village?

Enough, she told herself. All of this wasn't helping her get free. She had to concentrate on *escape*, at least for the moment, and figure a way out of this.

But as she began to pick through plans, a voice spoke up from what felt like a great distance, a voice she recognized: the boy who'd fought the Faceless with her.

"Lena, I'm so sorry this happened to you," he said, almost too quietly to hear. Either he was whispering, or whatever she was trapped in was muting sounds somehow. "But right now, I really need to know how to use the Spark. The king won't let you go unless I tell him how to use it."

The Spark? *That* was what he wanted to know? There was no way she'd ever tell him that, even if she *could* talk! Clearly the Spark could do more than heal, since it'd teleported her and Rufus. Who knew what else it could do? The last thing in the world she'd consider was handing its power over to the Golden King and letting him use it against the Last Knight and the rest of the Cursed City.

"Leave me alone!" she tried to yell, but no sound came out, and she inwardly growled.

"You know, this would be a lot easier if you turned her back," she heard the boy say, though this time it didn't seem like he was talking to her.

"Turn her back?" said a second voice, one that Lena recognized as the Golden King's, and instantly her anger doubled. "And why would you think I could do that?"

"*What?*" the boy shouted. "You turned all these people to gold, and have no way to bring them back?"

"Of course I don't. The glove only works one way, genie. Now, if you want this girl's freedom, *tell me how to use the Spark*."

Lena couldn't believe what she was hearing. She *had* been turned to gold, just like Rufus! So was she just a statue now? And the Golden King couldn't turn them back, at least not without using the Spark?

And what was this about a *genie*?

It was a term Lena had only heard once, while chatting with the Last Knight about the cauldron. He'd been telling her all about magic, including stories about a Wicked Queen and her spies, which she called the I's for some reason, apparently like the letter, which Lena had never understood. Maybe they didn't like working as a team? Anyway, one of them had almost started a war between a fairy queen and a genie that could have destroyed the entire world.

And that was what the boy was, a creature that could devastate everything? He looked human, but that didn't mean much; she of all people knew *that*. But if he was so powerful, why did he need the Spark to heal her? None of it made sense.

"Listen, Lena," she heard him whisper again, too softly for the king to hear from how far away the man's voice sounded, it seemed. "This Spark thing . . . it talked to me. There's something inside of it that wants *out*. If I touch it, it might get free, and then I have no idea what will happen. I'm not sure I'd be able to hold it back, or even if I'd want to, honestly." He sighed. "Maybe that'd be for the best? I could make this *all* go away, if I had the power. . . ."

Um, *that* didn't sound good, whatever he was talking about. But there wasn't much Lena could do about it either way.

"Yeah, I get that," he said, his voice still just a whisper, though now sounding more annoyed, and not really speaking to her anymore. "No, I know, I should just try to heal her with it, and see what happens. Yes, I *know* I could unleash something that might be dangerous, but . . . You don't have to tell me again. . . . Okay, you're *still* telling me. Could you *stop* for a second?"

There was no way he could talk to the Golden King that way. So either there was a third person in the room, or the genie boy was talking to himself. Neither possibility made Lena feel particularly good.

"Okay, Lena," he whispered, back to talking to her, apparently. "I think I figured a way out of this without making things a whole lot worse. I'm going to hold the Spark's bowl, then touch the flame to your statue hand. If you can hear me, maybe *you* can do whatever it takes to make it work. If that happens, heal yourself, and we'll all be better off. Then I can figure out later if I should set this magic free or not. So can you trust me, and just . . . make the Spark work? Turn yourself back human?"

Trust him? That was the last thing she'd do, considering who the boy worked for. Not to mention that if he *was* a genie, he'd been disguising himself as a human to hide his true self, and . . .

Well, okay, *that* she couldn't really hold against him. But still.

"Here we go," he said. "It's touching your fingers now. I hope you're in there somewhere and can hear me."

If the Spark *was* touching her, she couldn't feel it. But this might be her only chance to free herself, so whatever the boy's reasons, she didn't have much choice but to go along with him. She concentrated as hard as she could and turned her thoughts toward the Spark.

Please, turn me back to normal. And if you can, do the same for Rufus?

For a moment, nothing happened, and she began to worry that she'd done something wrong, or maybe the Spark couldn't hear her through the gold. But then light blinded her eyes, and she squeezed them shut quickly, wincing in pain. She tried to cover them with her hands but found she couldn't yet move them.

Opening her eyes, she saw the gold covering her body slowly disappearing, releasing first her arms, then her legs, freeing her far too slowly for her liking.

As the gold passed from her legs, she felt a wave of exhaustion hit her, and she collapsed, just as her feet returned to their regular, non-golden color. Taking a deep breath, she tilted her head and looked up at the boy who'd just saved her.

He stood over her holding the Spark, with the Golden King a few feet away, watching carefully.

"Uh, hello," the boy said. "We haven't really been introduced. I'm Jin."

"Hello, I'm Lena," she said.

Then she punched the boy as hard as she could.

The Spark went flying into the air as the boy crashed backward into the Golden King, knocking them both to the floor. She threw herself forward, in spite of her exhaustion, and caught the Spark before its bowl could hit the floor, then looked down at the boy angrily. "And it's *not* nice to meet you!"

CHAPTER 24

The pain from the Faceless's sword had been the worst Jin had ever felt. But getting punched across the room definitely came in second.

He slammed into the Golden King, knocking them both back against the wall with a huge crash. As they fell, Jin saw his hand almost touch the king's glove and instantly turned himself insubstantial the moment before he touched it. As the glove passed through him, he felt an odd sort of tingling from the magic and hoped he hadn't just turned *himself* into a statue.

"Rufus!" Lena shouted across the room as the gold covering the cat began to fade, just as it'd done for her. But it wasn't happening quickly, so they weren't going anywhere for the moment.

"Take the Spark from her, genie!" the king roared, pushing

right through Jin to get back to his feet. "Don't let her—"

A large chair slammed into him, and Jin looked up in surprise to find Lena searching for a second one to throw. "You should just learn to leave people *alone*!" she shouted, glaring at both Jin and the king, which seemed a bit unfair, since Jin hadn't done anything to her. Well, other than follow her around and try to find the Last Knight, but she probably didn't even know that. "No wonder everyone hates you!"

The Golden King's face contorted in shock and rage. *"No one hates me!"* he shouted, trying to push the chair off himself but only succeeding in turning it to gold, and therefore too heavy to lift. "I'm the most beloved chancellor to rule these kingdoms!"

Jin snorted, earning him a dark look from the king. "Oh, uh, sorry," he said, and quickly solidified, floating over to where Lena waited with her cat, who had just about finished de-golding. She aimed a small couch at him, but he put up his hands in surrender. "Wait, Lena! There are hundreds of Faceless just outside the door, so you can't escape!" At least not *that* way, he left unsaid, hoping she got the point. "If you hand over the Spark, I'm sure we can work something out where you and your evil cat go free."

Her eyes widened. "What did you say about Rufus?"

Jin winced. "I said the, um, *weevil* cat! Because he's cute as a bug, obviously."

"You're lying now, and you were lying before," she said, glaring at him. "You're a genie, and you work for the king!"

Okay, whoops, maybe she *did* know about the whole following-her-to-the-Last-Knight thing. "I wouldn't call it 'working' for him," Jin said, shrugging apologetically. "It's a whole servitude thing, but believe me, if I could get out of it, I would. I hate him too—urk!"

Jin's throat began to close, and he turned to find the king squeezing two fingers together. "Get to the *point*," the king growled.

"Right, the point," Jin croaked, and the king thankfully released him. Jin put up a hand for everyone to just pause for a moment as he took in a deep breath, though in truth, he had no idea what to say or do next. If Lena was going to get out of this unharmed, he was going to have to figure out a way to help her without the king realizing it. And that was going to take some finesse.

Sounds like you're in trouble, then.

Not helping! Jin yelled at the cosmic knowledge, then turned back to the girl, who'd now grabbed a six-foot-tall candelabra and was aiming it at Jin like a spear. "Lena, I could take the Spark from you if I wanted," he said, hoping she believed it. "Like you mentioned, I'm a genie. There's nothing I can't do. But I don't want to. I want you and your cat to leave here in peace. And that can happen, as long as you hand the Spark over, and tell us how to use it."

There. That should convince the king he was following orders.

Lena didn't respond at first, and while she considered things, Jin looked beyond her surface again, to see if he could get a sense of what she was thinking through her inner magic. The blinding blue that was her inner self still shone too brightly to look at directly, and he had to shield his eyes a bit, but there was more of the painful red color now too, running through the blue like cracks in a vase.

"I *can't* let you have it," she said finally. "The giants will come looking for it, and they'd destroy every human they came across until they found it."

"Show me how to use the Spark, and the giants will never threaten anyone *again*," the king said, now out from under the golden chair. "I'll destroy them *all* with its magic!"

Jin winced. Even though that sounded reasonable to him, he

didn't see Lena going for it. In spite of her incredible strength, the blue inside her wasn't the color of someone who wanted to see others destroyed. It was far too peaceful.

As he'd feared, Lena looked both shocked and terribly offended. "You won't *touch* them! They've done nothing to you. They just want their treasure back!"

"He didn't mean *destroy*," Jin said quickly. "He meant exile!" Another large red crack appeared in her blue light as he said it, and he flinched, hating that he was making things worse, though he wasn't sure what had set it off. The word "exile"? "I mean, he'll send them somewhere where they can be happy and free! I'm sure there are plenty of unoccupied clouds in distant lands or something."

"Enough of this!" the king roared. He stepped closer to Lena with his golden glove outstretched. "Give me the Spark, girl. I tire of these games."

"Stay back!" Lena shouted, and swung the candelabra, only for the king to catch it in his golden glove. The force of the blow made the king yell out in pain, but it didn't stop the glove's magic from working, as gold flowed up the candelabra almost too fast to see. Lena dropped it just before it could reach her hand, at least.

Jin let out a huge breath with relief. He'd freed her from being a statue once, but he doubted the king would allow them to use the Spark a second time. The Golden King liked his trophies too much for that, especially those of some particularly annoying heroes he'd turned to gold years before—

"Guards!" the king shouted out, as Lena was now defenseless. The doors opened, and a squad of Faceless entered the room, each holding one of the shadow-magic swords that had caused Jin so much pain. He instinctively floated out of their way, but Lena didn't look the slightest bit intimidated.

"I took down more of you than this in the forest," she said, putting her fists up, ready to fight. "You should give up now, before you get hurt."

"**Master,**" one of the Faceless said from the doorway, its voice echoing in the armor. "**We have news. We have found the hiding place of the Last Knight**—"

"The what?" the Golden King shouted, turning around in surprise.

"No!" Lena shouted, and Jin cringed. He didn't need the king knowing she had anything to do with the Last Knight, not while she was still in his power.

But the Golden King seemed not to have noticed. "That's

perfect!" he said to the Faceless. "Soon we'll have both the knight *and* the Spark. Now, bring the flame *and* the girl to me, whatever it takes!"

In response, the Faceless all turned in unison to aim their swords at Lena.

"You're *not* taking the Spark!" she said, narrowing her eyes. She took a step forward, ready to punch the knights through the walls, then stopped, looking away in confusion. "What is . . . *uh-oh*."

Uh-oh? Jin frowned, not sure what she was talking about. But a movement out of the corner of his eye caught his attention, and he turned to find one of the paintings sliding back and forth on the wall. He stared at it curiously before noticing that the furniture was shaking too. He hadn't noticed because he was floating in the air, but the entire castle seemed to be rocking slightly.

"What is this?" the king shouted. "Who would dare?"

"It's the *giants*!" Lena shouted back, her face filled with horror. "They've come down to the ground, looking for the Spark!" She hurried to the nearby window as Rufus tried to hide behind the remaining furniture.

Jin blinked. He didn't sense the giants anywhere close. How big and heavy *were* they to shake the land this much, even from some great distance?

"Which way is the mountain?" Lena shouted over her shoulder. "I need to see how close they are."

"What mountain?" the king asked.

"The *big* mountain, near the Cursed City!" she shouted. "I don't know its name!"

And just like that, Jin saw his chance. He hated to do it, but if she and her awful cat were going to live through this without being turned to gold, he had no choice.

Stupid spell, making me care! he shouted internally.

You really have to give that up already.

As he cursed out the cosmic knowledge in his head, Jin extended his arm down behind Lena's back, snaking it until he could just reach the Spark without her noticing. Before she realized what was happening, he grabbed the bowl the fire danced in and yanked his arm back up, the Spark now his.

"No!" she shouted, and leapt straight up in the air at him. Before she could reach the Spark again, he teleported it to another part of the castle, safe in an unused room, then turned insubstantial, allowing her to pass right through him and land on the other side. "I need to give back the Spark, or the giants will destroy everything they find!"

"It's too late for that!" he shouted back. "Go! Get out of here, *now*!"

Lena started to say something, but the ground shook again, reminding her of what was coming. Her eyes flashed between Jin and the window, a devastated look on her face, and for a moment she didn't seem to know what to do. Then, as the Faceless pushed forward, she let out a cry of frustration, then punched an enormous hole right in the castle wall.

"You *monster*!" the Golden King roared, stalking toward the girl. "You *dare* touch my castle?"

But before either the king or the Faceless could get close enough to stop her, Lena leapt onto Rufus's back, and together they disappeared out the hole in the wall in a blur.

A blur that Jin actually recognized now. The cat had Seven League Boots on. Smart of her. They'd never catch her now.

With Lena away, and safe—other than from the impending giant invasion—Jin turned back toward the king, then floated down to the floor, knowing he couldn't stop what was coming next.

"Well, I got the Spark back, as requested," he said to the raging Golden King, teleporting the Spark back from where he'd momentarily hidden it. The king didn't respond, looking too angry to even speak, so Jin continued nervously. "So, does that count as an official wish granted, or . . . no?"

CHAPTER 25

Lena and Rufus reappeared at the base of the mountain that led up to the giant village in the clouds, and Lena jumped off her cat's back, her heart racing so loudly she could hear it in her ears.

A foot the size of the Boot-ique crashed down just a few yards to her right, sending her and Rufus flying. Her cat meowed indignantly, trying to run uselessly while in midair, but she managed to grab him and hold him tight right before they slammed into a boulder on the side of the mountain, dislodging it with the force of the crash.

"Are you okay?" she asked him, releasing Rufus so he could stand back up.

"Lena is scared?" he asked, his whiskers twitching as he

looked up with fear in his eyes. "If Lena is scared, we go hide?"

She tried to smile reassuringly at him, but she found she couldn't even fake it. "I *am* a little scared, but we can't hide right now, little man. We have to turn my people around before they hurt someone!"

She craned her neck backward to look up at the giant, not recognizing him or the one on the mountain above, climbing down slowly with a third giant behind him. Each one wore the armor of the king's guards, which meant they were heading to war.

Only, they had no idea what they were getting into. Coming after the humans with so much ill intent meant they hopefully would never find the Cursed City. But that didn't mean they couldn't cause enormous amounts of damage to the kingdom all around it.

And then there was the matter of air sickness, this far down. Lena hadn't ever experienced it herself, so she wasn't sure how long it'd take to affect them, but she'd heard enough stories about the thicker air near the ground that did strange things to a giant's brain. The giants who lived on the ground permanently suffered from a complete brain fog, barely able to speak, let alone do anything other than cause trouble.

That alone explained so many of their problems with humans. If Lena herself only knew giants from their fog-induced rampages, she'd probably be terrified of them too.

Watching the giants climb down, she noticed something unusual: the mountain had gaps all the way up it to the summit, chasms that Rufus always had to leap over to make it up or down. But now she could see that the giants had created these gaps, as they were lined up perfectly for a giant's stride, giving them a good, solid place to put their feet as they climbed down.

How many giants had used the mountain that same way in the past? How often had they come down to the ground to ransack human villages and steal their magical items?

"Lena hides now?" Rufus asked, nuzzling her with his forehead. She absently scratched him behind his ears while trying to figure out what to do. When they couldn't find the city, they *might* head back up into the clouds, but more likely they'd just look for the next nearest human settlement. It wasn't close, from what Mrs. Hubbard had told her, but that wouldn't matter much to a giant, who could cover miles in minutes instead of hours or days.

A fourth giant reached the ground, one Lena recognized:

Creel, the Sparktender. He must have come to make sure the Spark was properly cared for. But if someone of his importance had come, then that meant—

A fifth giant slammed down, sending a wave through the ground that knocked Lena from her feet and forced Rufus to leap into the air. *"Humans!"* King Denir roared, shaking the few remaining trees still standing. "Give us back the Spark, or we will destroy each and every one of you!"

The *king* was here? Lena hadn't ever heard of him leaving the clouds before, especially not after the death of his brother, which had happened just before Lena was born. She couldn't imagine how mad he must be to have come down himself.

"Shouldn't we worry about air sickness, Your Majesty?" Creel asked. "I can already tell it feels thicker down here."

"That's a myth, Creel," the king said, shaking his head. "It's not real. Put it out of your heads and breathe in deeply, boys. We're going to destroy some humans!"

Lena felt sick even at the sight of the king, but maybe this could be a good thing. There'd be no way she could talk a king's guard out of their attack, but if she could just convince the king himself, he might turn the whole group of giants around.

Assuming he didn't try to throw a spear at her this time.

Fortunately, he didn't seem to be armed. But unfortunately, it wasn't like he needed weapons to just crush her with his feet.

"Your Majesty!" she shouted up at the king as loudly as she could. "Please, there's no need for this! We can talk—"

The king looked down at her briefly and squinted. His face contorted into a sneer as he seemed to recognize her, then lifted his foot up over her head. Realizing what was coming, Lena grabbed Rufus and leapt out of the way into the bushes to the side, even as the king's foot came crashing down, sending an earth-shattering shudder through the ground as far as Lena could see.

"Was that a human, Your Majesty?" Creel asked, not able to see Lena or Rufus from where he stood. "Did you get it?"

"I got *whatever* it was," he said. "The first of many. Keep moving. They'll have the Spark in this city of theirs, so we'll just have to demolish it so no human bothers us ever again."

Lena felt a wave of nausea pass through her. Not only had the king just tried to squish her without a second thought, but he didn't even think she was worth mentioning to the Sparktender. That was how little he thought of her.

You are no *giant.*

But no matter how much the king hated her, she couldn't

just let them destroy the city, or hurt any of the humans who lived there. She had to try to reason with him, *make* him listen, no matter what it took!

"They don't have the Spark!" she shouted, leaving Rufus in the bushes to catch the king's attention again. "If you'll just hear me out, Your Majesty—"

This time the king kicked out at her, crashing his boot into the forest just over her head. Hundred-year-old trees went flying in every direction, destroying any cover Lena might have had. Realizing this wasn't helping, Lena leapt over to where Rufus lay hiding, grabbed him, and moved farther around the mountain, hoping the rocks might hide them until she could think of something else to try.

"Another human, Your Majesty?" another guard asked.

"Indeed," the king said. "I don't hear it yelling anymore, though, so hopefully it's gone now. Horrible little monsters, humans."

"What was it saying?"

"Something about stealing the Spark, I think," the king said. "Do you see the city?"

The other guards all turned around, looking for the Cursed City, but seemed to have no luck. Lena felt her first bit of relief

211

at that: apparently the spell on the city was still working, at least.

"Keep searching until we find it," the king ordered, and the five giants set off into the forest, each of their steps sending trees flying. Lena climbed onto Rufus's back and pointed him away from the giants for the moment, completely at a loss as to what to do.

The king had recognized her; she *knew* he had. But even if he hadn't, he wasn't going to listen to any human, either. She needed to make him understand that the humans didn't have the Spark, at least not the ones in the Cursed City! Maybe if she put on the Growth Ring, so she could face him at his own height?

Except that if she did that, the king and other guards could easily overpower her, five to one. They already didn't think of her as a real giant; why would they suddenly listen if she was their height?

It didn't seem worth the risk of her being captured, or worse. But that left her without any ideas. She needed *help*.

Fortunately, there was someone nearby who might be able to offer it.

"This way, little man," she said quietly to Rufus, and pointed him in a new direction.

Even without using his Seven League Boots, Rufus moved quickly and had them around the side of the mountain in no time. As she directed him to a semi-hidden cave right in the mountainside, he slowed down, then stopped completely, a few yards away.

"There are *many* someones here," he said, his whiskers twitching nervously.

Not sure what he meant, Lena jumped off his back and petted him reassuringly, then slowly walked to the mouth of the cave. The last time her cat had mentioned many someones, it'd been because the Faceless had surrounded them.

The cave was far too dark to see inside, so she pulled an Everpresent Torch from her infinite pouch and held it aloft, its eternal flame lighting the cave floor inside, revealing nothing out of the ordinary. She took a step forward, then another, deciding that maybe Rufus had smelled the Faceless elsewhere. . . .

And then she froze, the light shining off an empty helmet on the cave floor. A helmet, then another, and *another*.

Faceless helmets.

"Hello?" she said as loudly as she dared. "Is anyone . . . there?"

"Well, well, look who it is!" shouted a voice from inside, and Lena immediately brightened. A figure stepped into the light of her Everpresent Torch, clad entirely in silver armor from head to foot, with a closed visor hiding his face. But there was no doubt in Lena's mind who it was.

"Lena!" the Last Knight said, laughing inside his helmet as he carried empty Faceless helmets in either hand. "It's been a while. How did the ritual go? Did you get your real name finally?" He paused. "And what's with all the earthquakes? I hope that was you celebrating!"

CHAPTER 26

Jin slammed up against a wall, not able to breathe. He clawed at his throat, knowing it wouldn't do anything against the magic binding him to the Golden King, but not able to help himself.

"I honestly just don't understand," the king said, examining the Spark before him as he held up his ringed hand, pushing two fingers together to cut off Jin's air. "Why would you let the girl go? You *had* to know I'd punish you."

"Can't . . . *breathe*," Jin said, and the pressure around his neck released enough for him to speak. He slid down the wall, taking in as deep a breath as he could before answering. "I did it . . . because she's dangerous. You saw . . . what she did to the wall and . . . the Faceless."

"And you saw what I did to *her*," the king said, holding up

215

his golden glove. "*No one* is dangerous to me, especially not with shadow magic on my side! But now there's no way of knowing how to work this thing. If I could master it, I'd have all the magic I need and wouldn't even need to keep feeding the twins' shadows."

Feeding shadows? And there was another mention of the twins, the ones the Last Knight had been looking for. Who *were* they? What was he talking about? "I can tell you . . . how to work it," Jin lied. "You saw . . . me use it earlier. To change her . . . back from gold."

The king glanced up at him, raising an eyebrow, then strode over to where Jin lay slumped against the wall. He picked Jin up by his tunic and held him in the air as he stared the genie in the eye. "Well?"

"It's . . . me," Jin said. "The Spark responds to me, and me alone."

What are you doing? the cosmic knowledge demanded, which was odd, since if anyone should know, it would be the knowledge.

Trying to save my life, Jin thought back.

Oh, I get it: you have no plan whatsoever, and so are winging it. Badly.

Pretty much.

The king narrowed his eyes suspiciously. "That can't be true.

The girl could obviously use it, and she said it was a treasure of the giants. They must have figured it out as well."

"They were using it for healing," Jin said. "Same with the girl. That, anyone can do. But to access its true power takes someone made of magic, and after all your purges of magical creatures, I'm all you've got."

The king sneered, then tossed Jin back to the floor. "I don't believe it. *Tell* me how you interact with it."

Now comes the hard part, Jin thought. He looked up at the Golden King and shook his head. "Sorry, but no."

Without even turning, the king raised a hand, and instantly Jin was choking again. He resisted grabbing his throat helplessly, knowing there was nothing he could do this time except wait it out, if he wanted his bluff to hold.

It helped to remind himself that even if he was in awful pain, the Golden King couldn't do any permanent damage, since this wasn't Jin's true form. Or so he hoped, at least.

Except this time, the king *didn't* release him or even bother asking another question. In fact, a minute passed, and the room began to darken. As it did, the pain seemed to fade, and Jin felt his eyes close, wondering how everything had gotten so sleepy all of a sudden.

Just as he was about to fall unconscious, the magical force closing off his air disappeared, and he took in a deep, gasping breath.

"*Tell me* how to access the Spark's power," the king said again, his back still to Jin.

"I did . . . tell you," Jin gasped. "I'm the only—"

This time it felt like his entire body was in a vise, compressing in on itself in the most agonizing way possible. He didn't have bones, but if he had, they'd have broken under the pressure within seconds. Even without them, the pain was beyond anything Jin had ever felt, even worse than the shadow-magic sword of the Faceless, and he had to keep himself from giving in, admitting he didn't know how to use it either and that Lena was the only one who could.

If you tell him that now, he'll have no use for you, and that'll be it, the cosmic knowledge told him.

Don't you . . . think I . . . know that? he thought back. *But look how selfless . . . I am! I'm protecting . . . her!*

No, you're protecting yourself, but nice try, the voice said, and Jin cursed inwardly, even through the horrible pain.

The king let it go longer this time before again cutting it off abruptly. "This will be the final time I ask," he said, now turning to stare down at Jin, who found he'd knocked over a table in his writhing. He'd been in so much pain he hadn't even noticed.

"I don't . . . know *how*, but . . . it's made of . . . genie magic," Jin lied again, trying to look his most sincere. "So it only responds . . . to other genies."

The Golden King watched him for a moment, and Jin tried to prepare himself for whatever punishment might be next, knowing that there probably was no way to do that. If the king *really* wanted to hurt him, he could: ownership of Jin's ring gave the king the power to do whatever he wanted to ensure that Jin fulfilled his wishes. He might even use one of his remaining wishes to make Jin cause himself damage somehow.

"Show me," the king said finally, and Jin let out a huge sigh of relief. For the moment at least, he was safe.

Now all he had to do was figure out a way to bluff through his lies.

Jin raised a hand, and the king passed the Spark to him.

Okay, magic, he thought at the flame, hoping he'd figure it out *very* quickly. *All you have to do is show off a little, and we can both get out of this. Help me out, and I'll do what I can to free you, like you asked.*

219

YOU MUST EMBRACE MY POWER TO FREE ME, the voice responded in his head.

Right, sure, that, Jin thought back, getting nervous as the king shifted impatiently. *But in the meantime—*

THERE IS NO "MEANTIME." TAKE THE POWER THAT IS YOUR BIRTHRIGHT, JIN. DO NOT LET A LESSER CREATURE CONTROL YOU, NOT FOR EVEN ONE MINUTE LONGER.

Jin sighed, finding it hard to disagree with that.

Jin, you'll regret doing this, the cosmic knowledge said in his head. *You have no idea what you're getting into here.* I *don't even know. The Spark is hiding itself from me, and that shouldn't be* possible. *I can't sense its true nature.*

Well then, you don't know if it's all that bad, do you? Jin thought back, realizing he'd made up his mind. However terrible the Spark might be, having its power meant he could free himself from the Golden King, and right now that seemed like the best idea in the world.

EMBRACE MY POWER, CHILD, the Spark repeated, and Jin took in a deep breath, then nodded.

Okay. I embrace your power. Let's do *this.*

The flame burning in the bowl instantly ignited into a

blazing inferno, rising a dozen feet in the air as the Golden King stepped away in alarm. "What are you doing?" he roared at Jin, holding up an arm to shield himself from the fire.

"Just what you asked," Jin said, grinning slightly in spite of the pain still radiating through his body in several places. That'd be easy to fix in a moment, though, when he had access to his full genie magic. "I'm making the Spark work. Why, are you nervous?"

The flame leapt from the bowl to engulf Jin, and the light grew so bright that he couldn't see past it. His whole body burned with power now, and he couldn't help but laugh as he could feel the Golden King's fear, even from a distance. It was almost as if the Spark was setting his old self on fire, the one that couldn't access his real magic, the one who had to play by the rules.

And in return, it was making him complete, maybe for the first time ever.

He'd never felt so powerful, so able to do . . . *anything*. Was this what the older genies felt like all the time? Completely in control of the entire universe?

I could get to like this, he thought, rising into the air.

You have no idea what you're doing, the cosmic knowledge said. *This is* far *more dangerous than I suspected!*

Eh, what do you know, sum total of all knowledge? You're just annoyed I got my power before I was supposed to!

The light gradually faded, and Jin glanced at the king, curious to see what his newfound magic could do. While the Golden King's nervousness was clear, Jin looked past it, down through the blackness within the king's inner self, to even the molecules that made up the human. And the Spark within Jin gave him the power to manipulate those molecules, to cause the king just as much pain as Jin had felt a moment before.

This was the magic he'd been owed his whole life, the magic of a full genie. Every bit of Jin felt like it was ready to burst with power. He could remake the world in his own image or create a volcano inside this horrible little human, whichever he felt like.

Or maybe both!

And why stop with the Golden King? So many humans had irritated him over the years, getting in his way during wish fulfillments or just being annoying. Maybe they all deserved to learn a lesson too.

YES, TEACH THEM, the magic said in his head. *THEY NEED TO LEARN THE TRUE POWER BEHIND THEIR MAGIC!*

Jin started to agree, then paused. Sure, humans had been

bothersome, but he didn't *really* want revenge on them, beyond a petty prank or something. Where was all this rage coming from that he was feeling suddenly?

Was it really him, or had the Spark infected him somehow?

DOES IT MATTER? WE ARE ONE AND THE SAME NOW. TAKE YOUR REVENGE ON THE GOLDEN KING. SHOW HIM WHO HAS THE TRUE POWER IN THIS WORLD!

The Spark was hard to resist, and Jin lifted a hand to do just that, wondering why he was even fighting the magic. He *hated* the Golden King with all his heart, sure. But he also didn't want a *new* master, telling him what to do and who to torture for revenge.

DO IT, the Spark commanded, pushing harder with its power, and Jin found his defenses weakening. He looked at the Golden King and felt hate flow from every pore. "You know what?" he shouted. "Let's see how you like it!"

And then he closed two of his fingers together.

Only, nothing happened.

The Golden King blinked, then slowly straightened up and smiled. He quickly closed his own fingers, and Jin found himself choking once more, even with the power of the Spark.

You have the power now, the cosmic knowledge told him, *but genie magic still binds you to the ring, to our laws, and you haven't broken free from that. The king is still in control of you!*

Um, whoops. Well, *that* wasn't good. All this power, and he was still helpless before the king. And what was worse, the human knew it.

NO! the magic shouted. *WE SHALL NOT BE MADE TO SERVE YET AGAIN. BREAK FREE OF THE GENIE BINDING AND YOU WILL BE THIS WORLD'S MASTER!*

If you do manage to free yourself of the genie spell, the cosmic knowledge said, *the power you'd have to unleash might destroy the world. Are you willing to do that?*

IT WOULD BE WORTH IT!

Jin winced, still not able to breathe, then slowly floated down to the floor, knowing he was in for new heights of pain.

But if the choice was either destroy the world, and everyone in it, or submit to the Golden King again, there wasn't much of a choice. Not when the idea of Lena getting hurt made Jin feel physically sick.

This isn't selfless, by the way, the cosmic knowledge said, sounding a bit smug. *You like her, so you're really doing this for yourself.*

For once, Jin didn't have the energy to argue. Instead, he gritted his teeth and bowed low before the king, still not able to speak.

"Now, my genie," the Golden King said, putting a hand on Jin's shoulder. "You still have a wish to fulfill, don't you? And your newfound power should make it easy. Now, *I wish for you to bring me the Last Knight*."

CHAPTER 27

Before the Last Knight could say another word, Lena leapt straight at him and hugged him so hard, the metal of his armor creaked in warning.

"I've messed everything up!" Lena shouted as she released her hug, leaving slight dents in the Last Knight's armor. "*Everything!* The giant king threw me out of the ritual because he knew I wasn't the same size as the others, even with my Growth Ring, so I came down here looking for you and Mrs. Hubbard's cauldron so I could use it to become my true size, but then this boy got stabbed by the Faceless, and to save him, I brought him back to the Spark for healing, only it turned out he's not a human boy, he's a genie, and he works for the Golden King, who took the Spark from me, and the giants want it back, so they're coming to destroy the Cursed City because they think humans took it!"

The Last Knight tilted his head, listening carefully. "Huh! I've apparently missed some things. But there's nothing there that can't be fixed."

"Really?" Lena said, stepping back in surprise. "You're not worried about all that?"

"Oh, it's concerning, of course," the knight said, and she could almost hear him smiling. "But I'm sure we'll figure it all out."

Lena just shook her head, astonished at his confidence. Still, it did make her feel better, letting her relax just enough to notice the Faceless's helmets in his hands. "Are *you* okay?" she said, nodding at them. "Did you get attacked?"

He shrugged, dropping the helmets. "Oh, I suppose you could call it that. But really, it was just some good exercise. I'm getting a bit out of shape, to be honest." He patted the armor around his stomach. "Soon I might not even fit into my armor! Too many of Ralph's cookies, probably."

Lena smiled at that, though she personally refused to eat any of Mr. Ralph's cookies, considering *he* was made of gingerbread, and it always struck her as weird. Before she could respond, though, the ground shook with more giant footsteps. "So what should we do? How can we stop the giants?"

"We, as in you, need to go back to the city and warn people what's coming," the knight said, putting a hand on her shoulder. "Meanwhile, *I'll* take care of the giants, the Golden King, and your genie friend, in that order. Trust me, I've been dealing with giants my whole life. Shouldn't be a problem."

Lena's eyes widened. "But you'll need my help! You don't know the giants like I do, and the Golden King has the Spark! If he figures out how to use it—"

The knight gave her what she assumed was a kind look, even if she couldn't see it through his helmet, which he never took off, to keep his identity a secret from the Golden King. "There's no one I'd rather have fighting next to me, Lena—you know that. But you've been through enough today, and the Golden King wouldn't even be involved if it weren't for me. Don't you worry, I can take care of all of this." He reached over his shoulder and pulled his crystal sword with its swirling white light out of a dark blue scabbard. "This is all I need, really."

"That's just your 'I' sword," Lena said doubtfully. "I know you said it's powerful, but . . ."

"First of all, it's the sword of the I's," the knight said, apparently just repeating what *she* had said, so making no sense. "And second of all, trust me, it'll be fine. I swear, these aren't the first giants I've faced." He snorted. "Not even close. It's just a thing with me, apparently."

Lena felt her heart begin to slow, in spite of the ground still shaking. Even if he was exaggerating, just having the knight here and promising to take care of things made her feel so much better. Ever since she'd met him, on her first trip down the mountain, the knight had been such a calming presence to her, somehow instantly understanding what it was like to be a small Lena in a land of huge giants. Even Mrs. Hubbard hadn't gotten it as well as the knight had.

And he'd been the first one to offer her the cauldron, and she'd almost taken him up on it, before worrying what she might turn into. He never judged her for saying no, either; he just wanted her to have the option, he said.

It was almost like the Last Knight had been a member of the family, right along with her parents. But unlike them, the knight was happy to help her fix things with the other giants instead of hiding her true size. That alone endeared him to Lena, even if he hadn't been so great in other ways.

"*Thank* you," she said, giving him another quick hug, which made him groan in pain this time. "I feel so much better just knowing you're here."

"Oh, I'm not going anywhere," the knight said. "Now, I should—"

And then he disappeared in a puff of smoke.

It took her a moment to even process that. "Mr. Knight?" she said quietly, reaching a hand out to where he'd just been standing. "*Please* tell me you just turned invisible with your 'I' sword?"

No one answered, and just like that, all the worry and guilt Lena had felt a moment before came flooding back, only now ten times as bad.

"The night left?" Rufus asked, sniffing at the air. "The smoke smells like the boy."

Lena's eyes widened. The *genie* had done this? Of course he had! Jin had probably been following her here to find the knight, after all. And now she'd led him right to his goal! He was probably here right now, invisible too!

"Jin, *give him back*!" she shouted, grabbing the compass needle from her pouch and swinging it around. But either Jin wasn't there, or he wasn't responding. Her compass did pull her to her right, back in the direction she and Rufus had come from, which made sense: Jin must have brought the knight back to the Golden King's castle.

Without another thought, she leapt up onto Rufus's back and pointed him in that direction. "We have to go back to the gold place, little man," she whispered. "Can you take us there as fast as you can?"

Before he could move, though, several trees came flying in their direction, and Rufus had to leap out of the way. "You're going the wrong way!" roared one of the giants at a second one, the giant who'd just kicked a bunch of trees at Lena and Rufus. "Why do you keep turning around?"

"I *didn't* turn around," shouted another giant. "You two got in front of me somehow!"

"There's got to be a misdirection spell," said a third, and Lena felt her body go cold. "That must be how the humans are hiding the Spark from us. Maybe we can overpower it?"

She bit her lip, even as Rufus slunk nervously to the side and out of the clearing created by the flying trees. If they went to rescue the knight, and the giants found a way to break the Cursed City's protective spell, the whole city could be destroyed before they got back.

But if she didn't help the Last Knight escape, the Golden King might turn him into a statue!

The guilt over causing all these problems for her friends felt like a wave, crashing over her head again and again until she couldn't breathe, but she had to push past that: the longer she took to figure out what to do, the more likely it was that she'd be too late for either choice. She needed to do *something*. But what?

Don't you worry, I can take care of all of this, the knight had said. And even if Jin had brought him back to the Golden King's castle, the knight would still have his "I" sword, which he was always bragging could turn him invisible or make him move really fast. She didn't exactly get it, but supposedly it'd come from some magical queen or another.

But even if he didn't have his sword, Lena knew what *he* would tell her to do: save the Cursed City first, no matter what happened to him. Because that was just who the Last Knight was.

Ironic, since he absolutely hated being called that name to begin with and always told her to call him by his real name. She still found it awkward, calling him—

The ground rumbled again, interrupting her thoughts, and she shook her head, knowing what she had to do now. "Okay, little man," she said to Rufus as the giants oriented themselves back toward the Cursed City and set about trying to break the spell. "We're going to go back to Mrs. Hubbard in a moment, okay? We have to warn everyone in the city."

"And treats!" Rufus said, looking up at her with excitement in his eyes. "Treats for *all*!"

"Let's hope so," she said. "But before we go, there's something I need to grab from the cave here. Mrs. Hubbard said the Last Knight had it with him, so let's hope she was right."

CHAPTER 28

A man in silver armor holding a familiar-looking crystal-like sword appeared in the middle of the Golden King's throne room, and though he had his helmet's visor down, Jin could still tell the Last Knight seemed disoriented, at least more so than when he'd last appeared in the king's castle.

Of course this time he wasn't here by choice . . . and *was* here in person, instead of just his image.

Out of curiosity, Jin looked past the Last Knight's armor to the magic within, only . . . he couldn't find it. Was the armor itself deflecting his senses somehow? Or was there something else that Jin was missing?

"Ah, Your Majesty," the Last Knight said to the Golden

King, bowing low. He straightened up, then aimed his translucent sword directly at the king, and it began to swirl with some sort of black light. "I see you missed having me around. Honestly, it was nice of you to bring me all the way here, even if you could have just sent a message, and I'd have come right over. It does seem like the time to end this little war we've been having, doesn't it?" The playful tone dropped from his voice, and he stepped closer to the king. "Now, give me the *twins*."

"Genie!" the Golden King shouted, holding his golden glove up toward the knight. "You were supposed to bring him here *captured*, in chains!"

"Oh, whoops, was I?" Jin said, slowly smiling. "You didn't mention that the most recent time you wished for it. Anyway, you've got one wish left if you want me to throw him in chains, though!"

"Don't bother wasting that wish," the knight said, after briefly glancing at Jin. "It won't help you."

And then he disappeared. Or he would have, if Jin had normal, human vision. Instead, Jin watched as the knight moved too fast for a human to follow, almost leaping between seconds, to sweep over to the king and put his sword to the man's throat, slowing back down as he did.

"Oh, this feels familiar!" the knight said, the sword getting even darker now.

"What . . . *release me*!" the Golden King shouted, his face pale with fear against his golden clothes. He tried to grab for the sword with his gloved hand, but the knight slammed his fist into the king's shoulder, and the Golden King shouted out in pain, his arm going limp at his side.

"Really?" the Last Knight said, then laughed. "Did you think that would work, honestly?" He nodded at Jin. "*This* guy, huh? I'm sorry you've had to serve him for so long."

"Well, he does have one wish if he wants me to stop you," Jin said, still grinning. "But then I'd be free of his service, so I hope he puts some thought into it."

The king went silent, his eyes darting all over the room as he considered. The knight let him for a moment, then used the hilt of his sword to knock the Golden King's crown from his head. "That's better," the knight said. "The whole point of having the people choose their chancellor was that a king *wouldn't* rule over them, and now look at what you've done. The princess who came up with this idea would be so disappointed in you."

The king growled in annoyance. "Would she? Why not ask her yourself? She's right over there, with her friends." He nodded at the golden statues closest to the throne, and Jin glanced over in curiosity. Sure enough, his new power from the Spark gave him access to the knowledge that was his birthright—

Except you haven't earned *it*.

—letting Jin find out quite a bit more about each of the cursed statues that he'd seen a thousand times but never bothered looking at closely. The four the king pointed at *were* royalty, though from what Jin could see of their histories, all four had given their kingdoms up, allowing whoever the people chose in the Choosing—the election for chancellor—to rule over them instead.

Each of the four statues also had odd bits of magic about them, something Jin had never noticed. The first woman, the princess the knight had been talking about, wore a pair of crystal slippers on her feet, somehow still translucent even after the rest of her had been turned to gold. The next two, a man and a woman, had vines wrapping up around their legs, thorny, ropy vines that seemed to come from nowhere.

And the fourth—

"Oh, *there* they are," the knight said, his playful tone hiding a bottomless pit of anger, from what Jin could tell. He might be pretending he didn't care, but this man *hated* the king for what he'd done. "I've been trying to free them for years, and you've had them *on display?*"

"Of course," the king said, sneering. "*They* were the famous faces of your whole pathetic rebellion, the ones the people told stories about. The sleeping princess, the prince who slayed giants, the girl who destroyed the Wicked Queen . . . the people listened to them, trusted them." He tried to twist and look over his shoulder at the knight. "But were you even on their side? We've all heard the rumors that you once *served* the Wicked Queen."

Jin's eyebrows shot up. The Last Knight had served the Wicked Queen, the woman who'd almost taken over the world twelve years earlier?

Not to mention the last wielder of the shadow magic, the cosmic knowledge told him.

Really? Now *that* sounded interesting. The rebel knight had been on the other side?

"You seem to know a lot about me," the Last Knight said, his anger now less hidden than before. "But I know quite a bit about you, too, *Midas*." The king looked startled at the sound of his real name. "How's your sister doing? Still hiding from you, thinking you'll turn her to gold as well?"

The Golden King growled softly. "Don't even *speak* of her to me. She's worth a thousand of you!"

"Oh, so she's got it wrong?" the knight said. "Maybe I should let her know that, the next time I see her. She's been aiding the rebellion, trying to take you down, you know. But that's probably only because you turned the rest of her family to gold, right?"

Jin and the knight both turned to look at the statues of the king's brothers and father behind the throne.

"Enough of this!" the king shouted, his face red with rage. "What do you *want*?"

"You *know* why I'm here," the knight said, sounding far angrier than before. "Where are the *twins*? The shadow children?"

Jin blinked. The twins . . . were children? Human children, or something *made* of shadow? Were they related to the Faceless's shadow-magic swords?

"Oh, they're safe," the king said, grinning as he turned to look at Jin. "I moved them to the shadow kingdoms in the south after your last appearance here. They're currently feeding

239

the shadow magic with the power of all the magical creatures I rounded up. The shadows grow stronger every single day. Soon they will sweep across this land, bringing fear wherever they fall, and I will no longer need to bother with this *chancellor* nonsense. Instead, I will *rule* everything—"

This time, the knight hit the king's bare head with the hilt of his sword. The king roared in pain, but the knight just shrugged. "Last question. Where's the object that controls the genie for you? Hand it over, or next time I'll use the blade of my sword."

Both Jin and the king looked down at the ring on the king's finger, and the knight nodded. "Ah, keeping it close. Smart. I would too. So much for that, though." And he reached around to take the ring off the king's finger.

Before he could, though, the king turned to Jin. "For my final wish," he shouted, *"I wish for more wishes!"*

For a moment, no one said anything. And then both the Last Knight and Jin began to laugh.

"What's so funny?" the Golden King asked, looking more angry at Jin than at the knight.

"Greedy until the end," the knight said, shaking his head.

"Right?" Jin said. "And nice try, Your Majesty, but you're *not* getting more wishes. It doesn't work that way."

Actually, the cosmic knowledge said, sounding a bit smug, *it does.*

Wait, what? Jin shouted inside his head. *How does that wish count? It's a loophole! He only gets* three *wishes!*

Well, he did *only get three, but now he apparently gets more. Seems like something the elders would have made sure didn't fly, but here we are.*

Jin's mouth dropped open. *You're serious?*

When am I ever not?

No. *No no no no no.* This pathetic human was going to get *more* wishes just because no one had thought to make a rule forbidding it? That wasn't fair!

Why would you ever think any of this is fair?

Jin started to yell back, but gave up. The cosmic knowledge had a point: none of this was at all fair. But more wishes? He could be granting the Golden King's every desire for centuries to come!

If not the entire thousand and thirty-eight years you have left. You didn't ask him how many "more" is.

Jin winced, then sighed deeply. "Um, so as it turns out, I'm going to need a specific number of wishes—"

"As many as I want!" the king shouted.

"Oh, *come on*," both Jin and the Last Knight said at the same time.

"And for my fourth wish, I want you to chain this knight up and take his sword!" the king finished.

The knight didn't wait for Jin to fulfill the wish. He grabbed for the ring, too fast for the king to even see, but Jin was even faster, even if he would have preferred not to be. As the Last Knight tried to steal Jin's ring, Jin quickly magicked chains around the Last Knight and teleported the man's sword into his own hand.

The knight yelled in surprise, his hand just inches from the ring, then toppled to the floor, chains wrapped around every inch of his armor.

The Golden King, now freed, dusted himself off, then leaned over the knight, sneering down at him. "You're going to be the *treasure* of my collection, do you know that? I hope you enjoy living the rest of your life as a golden statue. But first? Let's see who you've been all along."

And with that, he reached down and tried to pull off the knight's helmet.

Oooh, *that* was interesting, considering the knight's armor had messed with Jin's reading of the man, so he leaned forward to see what he could tell without the helmet on. But his movement caught the king's eye, and the man shook his head. "*You* have more wishes to fulfill. Why don't you start with removing the Cursed City's misdirection spell? They need to pay for harboring this rebel for so long."

"No!" the knight shouted. "There are *giants* looking for the city. If they find it, they'll raze it in seconds!"

This made the king's smile widen. "You heard the rebel," he said to Jin. "I wish for the Cursed City to no longer be hidden. Let it be revealed to *all!*"

CHAPTER 29

Lena and Rufus reappeared in the middle of the Cursed City, only to find themselves on the edge of a massive crowd. Almost everyone that Lena knew from the city was gathered around a stage where Pinocchio, the former chancellor, was addressing them, even as the ground shook constantly with the giants' steps, throwing them all around.

"I know you're all worried about the giants!" he was saying, trying to keep his footing as even some fairies watched nervously from a nearby rooftop. "I am too! But there's no reason to panic. We know the misdirection spell is still working, as it appears to be sending them in circles. I want to make it very clear that as long as the spell holds up, we're all completely safe!"

His nose began to grow, and he cursed, smushing it back into his face.

"He's lying!" someone shouted.

"I am *not*!" Pinocchio said, shaking his head. "My nose just takes things far too literally. We *are* safe here. They can't get through the misdirection spell!"

His nose grew again.

"Tell us the truth!" someone else shouted.

"Stop lying to us!" said a third human.

"Cut off his nose!" said a fourth.

"Whoa!" Pinocchio said, putting his hands up defensively. "Let's not get out of hand! I *am* telling the truth. We *should* be safe, as long as the spell holds. So the best thing everyone can do is go back to your homes and wait this out, because nothing on earth could disrupt the spell at this point, as we all know what a powerful witch Mrs. Hubbard used to be."

An enormous tree trunk flew through the air above them and crashed through several buildings just beyond where Pinocchio was speaking.

"Okay, we *might* be in trouble," the wooden man said, wincing. "Apparently the misdirection spell doesn't work on trees."

"They're destroying the town and we're all going to die, just like Pinocchio said!" someone shouted.

"What?" Pinocchio said. "I never—"

But he was quickly overwhelmed by the rest of the mob.

"We can't *leave*!" yelled someone else. "There are Faceless out there!"

"What's going to fall on us next, the *sky*?" yelled Lil, the chicken.

"It's going to be okay!" Lena shouted, pushing her way through the crowd to where Pinocchio was standing. Rufus, meanwhile, slunk to the back, not liking this many people around him. "Please, everyone, you need to listen to me!"

The crowd quickly went silent, as Pinocchio breathed a sigh of relief. "Good luck, Lena," he whispered to her as he leapt off the stage. "They're out for blood."

Pinocchio slipped out into the crowd, while Lena climbed up to where he'd stood and turned to the assembled residents of the Cursed City. "First, let me say that everyone is going to be fine," she said, giving the humans what she hoped was a calming smile. "Second, in spite of the Faceless, it *might* be a good idea if we all left the city and hid in the woods, *just in case* the giants do find a way through the misdirection spell—"

Apparently her calming smile didn't take, as the crowd

immediately burst into terrified screaming. "They *are* going to destroy the city! We need to run!"

"But then the Faceless will get us!"

"Why is all of this happening, Lena?"

She put up her hands for quiet, but the crowd was too riled up this time, forcing her to yell. "Someone . . . accidentally took something from the giants, so they've come down to the ground to take it back. But it's all just a big misunderstanding—!"

"A misunderstanding? They're *giants*! They want to eat us!"

"No one's going to eat anyone!" Lena shouted, not really sure if that was true. Yes, she'd heard the stories around the giant village about how humans were tasty, but she figured that was just talk. "Giants are just like you: they eat regular food, like pumpkins!" She pointed over at Peter's house.

"She's lying!" someone shouted. "My cousin was eaten by giants, I think! Either that or he moved, we were never sure."

"So they *are* going to eat us and destroy our city?"

"How are there even giants anymore? Didn't the Golden King send all the magical creatures away?"

Right, Mrs. Hubbard had mentioned that. One of the first things the Golden King had done after winning the Choosing and becoming chancellor was to round up all the magical creatures and exile them . . . somewhere. The Cursed City had welcomed anyone who'd come looking for refuge, but most had been taken by the king. "He might have, but those would have been giants who lived here, on the ground. The ones we're dealing with now come from above, in the sky!"

This actually made the crowd go silent for a moment. Someone snorted. "The sky? Do they fly around on little wings like the fairies?"

"Oh, stop it, George," said someone else. "Everyone knows clouds are like pillows, the most comfortable place to sleep anywhere. And that's where the Sun Giant lives. Of course there are giants in the sky."

"But none of us even knew there *were* giants up there! How could we have stolen anything from them?"

"How do *you* know all of this, Lena? Did *you* steal whatever it is they're looking for?"

At that last question, Lena sighed, knowing she didn't have any choice. She started to respond but then caught sight of Mrs. Hubbard standing near the back, a worried expression on her face as she looked Lena directly in the eye and shook her head back and forth.

Did she not want Lena to say how she knew the giants were coming? Yes, Mrs. Hubbard had told her all along that the other residents might not be okay with learning Lena was a giant, but this was a pretty special situation. She couldn't just *not* tell them, not if she wanted them to listen to her, to believe her.

There'd been enough hiding. They had to know the truth. *All* of it.

"I'll tell you how I know!" Lena shouted, and again they quieted down to listen, though there was still a little murmuring going on. "There's . . . something you should know about me."

Now even the murmuring stopped, while Mrs. Hubbard grew more animated, waving her hands dramatically to catch Lena's attention again. Lena nodded at her, trying to say she understood but had to do it, but that just seemed to egg Mrs. Hubbard on.

"You've all known me for years now," Lena said, hoping they'd remember that in the next few minutes. "And I'm friends with many of you. If we've never spoken, that's more my fault than yours."

The crowd muttered an acknowledgment to this, so Lena took a deep breath and dived in.

"But almost none of you know who I really am," she said

slowly. Another deep breath. "You see, I actually live—or *did live*—in the clouds above you too. I'm . . . well, I'm a giant. A tiny giant, but a giant."

And just like that, all the murmuring stopped dead as everyone stared at her in shock.

She laughed nervously. "Okay, now that the secret's out, I've got a plan to save everyone. The Last Knight has a cave—"

"You're no giant," someone shouted, sending a familiar feeling of nausea bubbling up from Lena's stomach.

"How could you be? You're so short!"

"She's only twelve. She's actually pretty tall for her age!"

"She'd be short for a *giant*."

"That's because she's clearly *not* one. She's obviously human!"

Suddenly the giants, the Spark, the Golden King, *none* of it mattered to Lena. All she could hear in her head was King Denir's voice, over and over.

You are no *giant*.

Her heart began to race as her anger rose. The crowd continued shouting out how they didn't believe her, and she started to feel dizzy.

You are no *giant*.

"Why would she lie?" someone shouted.

"Probably just wants to feel all special," someone else said. "Important. But she's not better than any of us. She's just some ordinary human, like we are."

You are no *giant.*

An enormous growl ripped from the depths of Lena's soul, and the entire crowd went silent. "I *AM* A GIANT!" she roared, stepping down from the stage. She turned, grabbed the wooden platform in her hands, then ripped it apart before the stunned mob, tossing both sides out and over the city walls. "As true a giant as ever *lived*! I don't care if you don't believe me. *I am a giant!*"

As quickly as her anger had come, it dissipated, especially before the frightened faces all staring at her in horror. With the rage gone, she was left feeling exhausted and embarrassed as she looked around at the humans who'd been her friends, who'd taken her in. "I'm . . . I'm sorry," she said. "But you need to listen to me—"

"She *is* one of them!"

"She's been a spy for the giants all along!"

"Get her!"

To Lena's shock, the mob began to surge toward her, and she backed away in surprise. Even many of her friends were on the attack, including Peter and some of the nutcracker guards.

"I'm not a spy!" she shouted as hands reached out for her. A cabbage came flying at her, thrown by a donkey, but she dodged, and it slammed into the ground next to Lil, who shrieked. "I'm your friend! And I can help save everyone, but we have to get out while the misdirection spell is still working!"

The crowd continued forward, ignoring her, grabbing for her . . . until a weird buzzing filled the air.

It was only there for a moment before disappearing, but Lena sadly thought she knew what had happened.

"The spell," she whispered, looking up in the direction of the mountain.

"I see it now!" shouted one of the giant guards, his voice echoing in the distance. "The human town, it's right in front of us!"

All eyes in the village turned up to the sky, where five giants, including the king, stared down at them from only a few miles away, the misdirection spell now either gone or no longer working.

"Destroy the city!" a second giant shouted.

"And we'll feast on them all for dinner!" shouted a third.

"These humans will pay for their crimes against giantkind!"

the king roared, and the other giants all began yelling in agreement. "Crush them all beneath our boots!"

"Oh *great*," said a tiny egg on the shoulder of the city's centaur doctor. "I *just* get fixed up, and now *this* happens? *Fantastic.*"

"*Time to panic!*" Lil shouted, and everyone began to scream and run in a thousand different directions.

CHAPTER 30

Not knowing what else to do, Jin decided to panic. As many wishes as the Golden King wanted? He could be serving the human for another thousand years!

Humans typically don't live for multiple centuries, the cosmic knowledge said, which Jin appreciated, but even that didn't improve his mood much. He'd only been alive for twelve years so far, so even *one* century was too many.

There has to be a way out of this wishes loophole! he thought as the Golden King's Faceless army gathered, preparing for Jin to teleport them, the king, and the chained-up knight all back to the Cursed City to watch it be destroyed. The king hadn't yet wished for it, but he'd made it clear that wish was coming, which meant there wasn't much Jin could actually do.

In the meantime, the king *had* wished for an elaborate siege engine, a tall wooden tower on wheels that normally would have been used to help attacking soldiers pass over an enemy's castle wall. But instead, the king had Jin modify it so that it was now basically a luxurious, compact throne room, perfect for viewing the giants' attack from on high.

With no need to hoard his wishes anymore, now he was just showing off, apparently.

As long as the king has your ring, he's in complete control of you, the cosmic knowledge continued. *You cannot harm him by your magic, but* he *can punish* you *as much as he likes.*

You can see how this whole system might not make a lot of sense! Jin yelled at the cosmic knowledge. *It was* way *too easy to take advantage of it all!*

True. But what better way to learn humility than to realize not all your assumptions are true?

Jin groaned loudly, drawing looks from some of the royals. It probably didn't help that he was floating in midair, either. Now that Jin had his full magic and the king had all the wishes he could ever want, there wasn't much reason to hide Jin's presence anymore. If anyone questioned the king keeping a genie around, the Golden King could just wish them away.

If only I could wish him *away.*

Again, you can't cause him any harm . . . not by your magic.

Not by his magic. Was the cosmic knowledge trying to point out a loophole of its own? Could Jin maybe arrange for a physical trap of some kind, maybe even send a dragon after the king, like he'd done when helping the king win the Choosing years before and become chancellor?

You could, but he could always just make you wish it away. You're probably thinking about this the wrong way.

Well then, tell me the right *way to think about it!* Jin yelled in his mind.

Oh, I couldn't do that. The cosmic knowledge sounded like it was enjoying all this way too much.

Meanwhile, that wasn't the only voice in his head, not anymore. The Spark had filled Jin with magical power, and the longer he carried it inside him, the more he could feel an anger against the world, a desire to rule over it . . . or *destroy* it.

YOU ARE A COWARD. TAKE THE MAGIC YOU'VE GAINED AND USE IT. DO NOT LET YOUR ELDERS CONTROL YOU LIKE THIS. YOU HAVE THE POWER TO BREAK FREE FROM THEIR RULES!

While that all *sounded* good, the part of Jin that *didn't* want to destroy the entire world by breaking the ifrits' rules figured giving in to the Spark wasn't the best idea. At the very least, he could leave it for a last resort, if things were really dark.

Maybe he could just grab Lena and make a whole new world if this one was destroyed?

Um, I feel like you're almost getting less *humble. And besides, if you defy the ifrits, they will come for you. They will not allow another renegade genie in this world.*

LET THEM TRY. TOGETHER WE CAN DESTROY ALL WHO OPPOSE US.

Jin sighed. *Okay, both of you be quiet,* he told them. *And, Spark, you need to tone it down, honestly. You take hating people to an uncomfortable level, even for me. And that's saying something.*

"Genie!" the Golden King roared, and yanked Jin over to his side using the ring's power. The king had taken his throne into the siege tower, with the chained-up Last Knight lying on the golden floor next to him. "The Faceless are ready, and we're missing all the fun. I hereby wish for you to transport my siege engine and the rest of my army of Faceless to the Cursed City, so that we might watch it be *destroyed*!"

Speaking of hating people, Jin thought, but bowed low to the king. "Your wish shall be granted," he said, rolling his eyes just to himself before using his power to send them all to the Cursed City.

The last time the genie had been to the city—somehow just a few hours earlier in the same day, even if it felt like months had passed—it had been busy yet peaceful, with its residents going about their lives without a worry, other than that annoying chicken and the fun Invisible Cloud of Hate lady.

Now it was like night and day.

"Run for your lives!" the man made of cookie was shouting, zipping around almost too fast for even Jin to see as he tried to carry people out the city's front gate. The nutcracker guards rushed through the streets toward the back gate, where a group of giants were taking their time, playfully kicking the walls down, laughing like children.

Air sickness, the cosmic knowledge said. *It's affecting them already. They're going to slowly lose their reason, the longer they're down here.*

But even as the townspeople fled the giants out the front gate, they now found their escape route blocked by the army of Faceless and the Golden King's siege engine.

"Back into the city!" Pinocchio shouted, waving everyone toward the center of the city. "Run, everyone!"

"Genie!" the Golden King shouted from his siege tower throne. "I wish you to set that puppet on fire for me!"

Jin cringed, then turned and floated to the fleeing puppet, who had now caught sight of Jin. *"You!"* the puppet shouted. "I know you! You're the one who told everyone that I was a puppet of the fairy queens during the Choosing!"

Jin shrugged helplessly. "Yeah, I'm sorry about that. I mean, it's not like it wasn't true, though, right?"

"Merriweather the fairy queen gave me *life*!" the puppet shouted. "That doesn't mean she, or any of them, controlled me!"

Jin winced. "That sounds questionable, but still not my business if you want to keep it hidden. Unfortunately, I had to fulfill a wish, then and *now*."

The puppet stared up at him, putting on a brave face. "You don't scare me," he said, his nose growing by an inch or two.

"If it helps, I don't want to do this," Jin said, though inside him, he could feel the Spark burning with desire to watch the puppet go up in flames. Whatever the Spark was, it wasn't the *nicest* magical fire. "And I'm sorry!"

Jin winced, then snapped his fingers. The poor puppet began to burn immediately.

Before Pinocchio could even yell out, though, Jin extended his arms toward the nearest rain barrel, grabbed it, and overturned it on the poor wooden puppet, instantly extinguishing the fire.

The puppet stared up at him in confusion, water dripping off his wooden limbs and clothes. "But . . . why did you save me?"

"He only wished for you to be *set* on fire," Jin said, smiling slightly. "Not for me to let you burn up, too."

"Cruel, and unusual," said a familiar voice, and Jin turned to find . . . no one. Oh, right, the Invisible Cloud of Hate. Using his magical senses, he could make out the transparent outline of what looked like a human woman. "I like that. The puppet always bugged me, but he didn't deserve to be burned."

"I didn't do it by *choice*—" Jin said, only to be yanked back to the side of the Golden King again.

"Clearly, I need to be more careful in my wishes, don't I, genie?" the king said, sneering at him. "I'll make sure to be very specific from here on out. Now, who shall be next?"

"Stop this!" the knight shouted at his side. "These are your subjects! You should be *protecting* them from the giants!"

"Oh, I'll slay the giants," the king said, nodding. "But only after they've destroyed the city. This town has hidden you rebels for too long, and there's only one punishment for traitors: *death*!"

"Wow, he's almost as bad as the knight is," said the Invisible Cloud of Hate, now apparently on the siege tower with them. "And I've hated the knight for half my life, so that says something!"

Jin blinked at that, while the king turned back to the city, looking for his next victim, only to stop as his eyes fixed on someone. "What is that horrible girl doing up there?"

Jin followed his gaze to where the giants had been wrecking the back gate of the city just a moment ago. There, on a flat rooftop, were Lena and her cat, preparing to face down the giants . . . *alone*.

See? the cosmic knowledge said in his head as Jin's mouth dropped open in surprise. *Now* that *is a selfless act!*

CHAPTER 31

Get her!" someone shouted, and the crowd turned back on Lena. "She's with the giants. Maybe we can hold her hostage!"

"I'm not with *them*—I'm trying to help *you*!" Lena shouted, but was soon overwhelmed by the villagers all grabbing for her, holding her to keep her from escaping. She tried not to hurt anyone as she pushed her way clear, but the sheer number of them made it almost impossible.

"You lied to us!" Peter shouted as he grabbed one of her arms. "And to think I've been living in a *giant's* pumpkin this whole time!"

"What did you think it was?" Lena asked him, pulling herself free. "It's literally a *giant pumpkin*! And the Boot-ique is a giant's boot!"

Someone else gasped. "We've been shopping in a giant's boot? The horror!"

"Out of the way!" shouted a familiar voice, followed by the slightly nervous growl of a six-foot-tall cat. Mrs. Hubbard came crashing through the mob on an anxious Rufus's back, trailed by a small group of tough-looking fairies, each one glaring at the mob. The shopkeeper held one of the giant toothpicks Lena had traded to her a few years ago. For Mrs. Hubbard, it was a perfectly-sized staff and usually helped her reach high things in the Boot-ique. Now she used it to prod, push, and poke various villagers in the behind whenever they didn't move out of her way fast enough.

"Lena!" Rufus shouted as they neared, and Mrs. Hubbard helped pull Lena onto his back. Her brave little boy swatted at a few members of the mob too, just to show his courage, but most were as intimidated by him as he was by them, so they gave him plenty of space.

"We need to get you out of here," Mrs. Hubbard said as Rufus hissed at the crowd, opening an exit for them back toward the Boot-ique, but also sending her little fairy defenders scurrying away. "Are you okay?"

"I'm . . . I'm fine," Lena said, still barely able to comprehend everything that was happening. She almost couldn't believe how quickly the city had turned on her, just because she'd told them the truth about her identity. Even her *friends*!

Part of her hoped that they were just terrified of the invading giants, so weren't thinking straight. That even sounded logical. But mostly she worried that Mrs. Hubbard had been right all along, and the humans just wouldn't ever accept a giant, even one their size.

And if that was true, then Lena truly had *nowhere* to go, no one who'd welcome her as she was. The thought scared her almost as much as the giants' attack.

They made it to the Boot-ique without too much trouble, as people seemed to be fleeing toward the front gate of the city, away from the giants. At the door to her shop, Mrs. Hubbard climbed off Rufus's back. "I have to gather the children and get them out of the city," she said. "Stay here, and we'll all go together."

Lena smiled down at her, wondering if this was the last time she'd see the woman who'd been almost a second mother to her. "I can't," she said, her voice cracking. "I have to . . . I have to *fix* this. It's all my fault."

"Lena, no!" Mrs. Hubbard shouted, but it was too late: Lena had already turned Rufus toward the back gate, where the giants had started kicking in the walls, reveling in the destruction. Lena hoped that was due to the air sickness, but if it wasn't . . . she didn't want to think what that said about her people.

As Rufus carried her through the crowded streets, leaping over residents and bouncing off the sides of buildings wherever there wasn't room to maneuver, Lena considered the only two options she could think of to help. Option number one, she could try surrendering, admitting that it was she who'd lost the Spark and promising to get it back. That had about a zero percent chance of working, especially after the king had tried to crush her in the forest.

That just left the second option: Mrs. Hubbard's cauldron, which she'd retrieved from the Last Knight's cave.

Back in the forest, she'd decided the Growth Ring wouldn't work, mostly because even with her giant strength, she'd be no match for the fully grown guards. But the cauldron would turn her into her *true* self, the self she believed she really was. If that was the case, and she could become a *true* giant in their eyes, maybe they'd finally be open to listening to her.

One of the outer walls came crashing through a building next to Rufus, and he leapt to avoid it. Fortunately, none of the debris struck any of the fleeing residents, but it was close and just going to get worse the farther the giants made their way into the city.

"We go with the people too?" Rufus asked, trying to reverse and follow the crowds, but Lena turned his head back toward the giants.

"No, buddy, we have to *save* everyone," she said, hoping her nose didn't lengthen like Pinocchio's. She just wasn't sure what possible chance they might have, even if she did grow to their size permanently. But what else could she do? The only reason the city was in danger was because of her!

"Lena is scared?" Rufus said as he was forced to climb up to one of the roofs to avoid a surge of residents. The rooftops were clear all the way to the back of the city and gave Lena a good view of the giants' attack, which they seemed to be enjoying even more now, to Lena's disgust.

"I'm terrified, little man," she told him, patting his neck. "But I think I can take it from here." She got down off his back on the roof and pulled the oversized cauldron out of her infinite pouch, stretching the pouch's opening far past its usual size just to get it free, then placed the black pot down on the roof beside her.

The cauldron's magic kept it filled with liquid, bubbling away but never spilling, even if you turned it upside down. Rufus seemed to recognize it from when he himself had grown, as he sniffed at the brew until Lena pulled him away. "You should go find Treats Lady and help her evacuate, okay? I want you to be safe."

Rufus turned to go, his whiskers twitching wildly . . . then stopped and came back to her. He nuzzled against her, looking down at the ground. "I help," he said quietly. "Even against the big ones. I stay with *Lena*."

Lena's heart rose into her throat, and she found she had no idea what to say. Instead, she just hugged him close, her tears getting lost in his fur. "I'll be okay, buddy," she said quietly. "But you'll be too small for this. Right now, I need to be *big*."

"Lena is *always* big," Rufus said defiantly, and she swallowed hard, almost losing it again. She hugged him a second time, tightly, hoping this wouldn't be the last time she saw him. "I help! I wear my collar again?"

He'd never argued with her this much. And if she did shrink him back down to normal cat size, he could stay with her, tucked in her pocket for safety. At least then she'd know he was okay. "Maybe you're right," she said, pulling his miniaturizing collar out of her pouch. "But you have to promise to stay in my pocket, okay?"

He nodded, and she wrapped the collar around his neck and started to fasten it, only to look back at the cauldron nervously. Yes, her plan might work if it did grow her to a normal giant size . . . but what if it didn't? What if King Denir was right, and she really *wasn't* a giant, not even on the inside?

Rufus was the only one she'd ever heard of growing from the cauldron. Everyone else had turned into something else completely, or had some inner aspect of themselves heightened, like the three goat brothers whose hatred of trolls grew so much, they had to leave the city to hunt them down under bridges.

But what choice did she have? If she used the Growth Ring again, they could easily just grab it off her finger, between the five of them. The only way she could make sure they listened to her was if she changed, permanently.

Lena took a deep breath, then closed Rufus's collar. He instantly shrank down to his past size, and she picked him up, setting him on her shoulder as she stepped over to the cauldron and looked down into its bubbling depths.

"You're a real giant," she told herself, clenching her fists. "You're a *real* giant, no matter what anyone else thinks. You *know* this is true."

She bent over and cupped some of the cauldron's liquid in her hands, and it came out warm to the touch. She bit her lip, then brought the liquid to her mouth—

CHAPTER 32

What is she *doing*?" the Golden King asked, glaring at Lena in the distance.

Jin squinted, changing his eyes to those of an eagle to better see. "It looks like she's messing around with an old cauldron of some kind."

"That's the Cauldron of Truth," the Invisible Cloud of Hate said. "*Old* magic. I wouldn't play with it if I were you. But then again, I'm *not* you, and I'm already stuck as basically a ghost, so what do *I* know?"

"Get over there," the king demanded. "Whatever she's doing, *stop her.*"

Jin winced but floated away obediently. This wasn't going to be an easy task, not with the spell that the girl had cast on him earlier—

Would you just admit you like *her already?*

Never! And it's a spell.

And because of that definitely-real-and-not-made-up spell making Jin feel biased toward her, he was going to have to figure out a way to make sure she wasn't harmed, while still fulfilling the king's wish.

Except the king didn't make *a wish. He just ordered you to go.*

Jin froze in midair, realizing the cosmic knowledge was right for once. The king had ordered him, but *not* in the form of an official wish!

Um, I'm always *right, actually.*

Well, that was certainly debatable. But if the king hadn't made a wish, then Jin didn't have to stop Lena at all and could actually make sure she was safe! All he had to do was—

"I *wish* for you to stop her!" the king yelled out from behind him, making Jin curse. *Fine*. He *would* stop Lena from whatever she was doing but still do his best to keep her safe.

As Jin approached, he saw Lena shrink Rufus, then move to the cauldron and dip her hands into it. She brought some of the liquid inside to her mouth—

And he froze her hands in place, then magically evaporated whatever had been in them.

"Sorry about this," he said as his face turned red. She looked up at him with surprise, only for that surprise to quickly turn to anger. "I didn't have a choice. I had to fulfill a wish."

He released her hands, and she immediately dove for the cauldron, making Jin stop her once again, this time with her head just a foot or so above the brew within. "Let me *go*!" she shouted, fighting against his magic with all her strength. She was struggling so hard, her feet actually created small ditches in the roof.

"I just told you I can't!" he said. "I really am sorry, though. But if you want to take out the Golden King, I'd be happy to look the other way?"

"The giants are going to destroy this whole city!" she shouted, pushing even harder now. "I have to drink from this cauldron and make myself their size, or they'll never listen to me!"

Jin raised an eyebrow. "Why would you want to be their size? It seems like it'd be good for destroying things, but not much else."

YOU DON'T NEED TO BE THEIR SIZE TO DESTROY, the Spark said in Jin's head, but he ignored it.

"I was supposed to be that big!" Lena shouted, gritting her teeth. "I'm a giant too, but I was born human-sized instead, so the king hates me and won't listen to a word I say!"

Whoa, really? Lena really *was* a giant, like Rufus had told Jin a few hours earlier? Maybe he owed the cat an apology. He glanced at the creature, who was looking up at him with an annoyed stare. Nah, the cat didn't deserve *anything*.

"That seems like the king's problem, not yours," Jin said with a shrug as the cat leapt down from Lena's shoulder to better glare at him.

"Well, it's my problem right now, because *you* took the Spark from me, and they want it *back*!" she growled. "If you gave it back to them, you might stop all this!"

Jin scrunched up his face, considering things. *Can we separate again?* he asked the Spark.

YOU AND I ARE ONE *NOW, AND INSEPARABLE, NO MATTER—*

"The Spark tells me that's not going to work," Jin said apologetically. "And the Golden King really wants to see this place destroyed, so I'm pretty sure he won't wish the giants away. But I might be able to get you out of here, and to safety. I'd even throw in the cat, if that helps?"

"Just let me *go*!" she shouted as the giants drew nearer. "People are going to get hurt!"

LET THEM.

273

Jin, the cosmic knowledge said, *she needs your help, but not with your magic.*

What does that *mean?* Jin asked, but the knowledge went silent, just like it always did after being vague. It was so irritating!

Not knowing what else to do, Jin swept the cauldron off the rooftop and down into the city, then released Lena from his magical hold. She cried out as the cauldron went flying and started to move after it, but Jin immediately blocked her.

"They're not going to listen to you, you know," he told her.

She growled loudly and threw a punch, but he went insubstantial before it hit. "You don't know anything about them *or* me!" she shouted.

"Maybe not," he said as another punch passed through his chest. "But I can *see* the inner you, and it's beautiful, giant or not. Why would you want to change yourself?"

"I don't want to change the *inside!*" she shouted, this time aiming for his head. "They don't care about who I am that way, just how I *look!*"

Jin blinked and changed himself into a Faceless, then Rufus, then Humphrey the egg, before morphing back into himself— making sure his height was the same as hers, of course.

"Speaking as someone who can look like anything, who cares what you look like?"

Her eyes narrowed, and she backed off slightly. "*They* do. The giants, all of them! My parents wouldn't even let me out of the house like this. I had to sneak out when they weren't paying attention. Giants *hate* humans, and that's all they see when they look at me!"

"Like I said, that sounds like *their* problem," Jin said. Flying debris from the giants' destructive attacks passed through him and went crashing toward Lena, who punched it away absently.

"The cauldron that you just *threw away* would have shown them all who I was," she said, her fists clenched at her side. "It brings out the true self of anyone who drinks from it."

"Oh, really?" Jin said, and smiled. "Then let me show you what it would have done to you, using the same spell as the cauldron."

Smoke filled the air around Lena for a moment, then dissipated in the wind, leaving her exactly the same as before.

She looked down at herself in surprise, then up at Jin anxiously. "This . . . is my true self?" she said quietly. "I didn't change, though!"

"Maybe that's because this *is* the real you," he said. "And you know what? I'm pretty sure you can take care of those giants at this size. You've got everything you need already."

Do you have any idea what you're talking about? the cosmic knowledge asked. *What does she have to fight the giants?*

Not a clue.

Right. And you didn't actually just cast a spell, either. You lied.

Well, you told me she didn't need magic *to help her!*

I didn't say to trick *her!*

I'm not, Jin said firmly. *This is no trick, no lie. She's who she is, and I bet she really* can *beat these giants.*

Lena was looking down at herself, then at Rufus, who rubbed himself against her leg, purring. "Lena is a giant, always," the cat said, and Jin decided maybe it wasn't as horrible a creature as he'd thought.

Lena swallowed hard, then bent down and ran a hand along Rufus's collar, lost in thought.

"So, does that mean you think I'm right?" Jin asked, not liking her silence.

"Shh," she said, reaching into a pouch on her belt for something. She pulled out a ring and looked at it next to Rufus's collar. "You might not be *completely* wrong."

That'd be a first.

Oh, be quiet.

She unfastened the collar from her cat, who grew back to his usual size, then considered the collar and the ring. "I think I have a plan," she said, looking up at Jin. "But I could use your help."

"Well, I *did* fulfill my last wish," Jin said, "so until I'm dragged back—"

And then he disappeared, yanked back to the Golden King's side.

"Did you stop her?" the king asked, glaring at Jin.

"Of course," Jin said, squinting back to find that Lena and Rufus had both leapt off the roof. "See? She's running away."

"Perfect," the king said, grinning. "I'll have you find her later, so she can be punished for what she did to my castle. But for now, let's enjoy the city's destruction!"

"Wow, seriously just the worst," the Invisible Cloud of Hate said. "He can't feel it, but I'm punching him over and over! Pointless, sure, but still, satisfying!"

CHAPTER 33

Lena knew Jin hadn't used any magic on her, of course. Or she was *pretty* sure, at least. She hadn't felt anything, first of all, and second . . . she didn't trust the genie farther than she could throw him now. And considering he had just been insubstantial, she couldn't throw him at *all*.

But that didn't mean the genie was wrong, not about who she really was, or hoped she was, or even about some other things. Things like how the other giants were the ones with the problem, not her.

The fact that they saw her as human wasn't due to anything she'd done—apart from accidentally taking the Spark, but even that had happened after the king had kicked her out of the ritual. And even their hatred of humans didn't make any sense, given who was destroying whose city at the moment.

Then there was the other thing Jin mentioned, that Lena had everything she needed to face the giants. It'd taken her a few seconds to realize it, but she had eventually come to understand what he meant. Or at least, come up with a plan.

Of course, if he'd stuck around, it would have been a bit more helpful, but she had a much more reliable friend at her side anyway.

Because if it *was* the giants with the problem, well, then maybe the way to solve all of this was to give them a little perspective.

And that was how Rufus ended up running through the empty streets in the back section of the Cursed City, looping around behind the attacking giants, with a few hundred feet of miniaturizing collar trailing behind him from his mouth.

Sure, the miniaturizing collar wasn't that size to begin with, but slipping the Growth Ring on it had done *wonders* for its size.

Holding the other end of the collar, Lena waited in the giants' path, dodging debris when she had to, as they destroyed their way farther into the city.

"Humans!" shouted the nearest giant, who Lena decided sounded like Creel, just a few dozen yards away now. "We eat all of you!"

The air sickness was really getting to them if even Creel had turned so violent. But that would all be fixed in a few moments.

"Eat them! Eat them!" one of the guards shouted.

"Horrible little thieves!" said King Denir, and Lena flinched at the sight of him but held steady. He needed this most of all.

The ground shook harder and harder with each step they took, and Lena worried that Rufus wouldn't be able to make it back. But there he was, sprinting around the other side of the giants, the collar still in his mouth. He looked terrified but hadn't run and hid, like Lena was sure he wanted to.

What a brave, courageous, *amazing* little man he was.

He skidded to a stop as he reached Lena and dropped the collar from his mouth. "I did it!" he said, purring softly, while still eyeing the approaching giants. "Lena is proud?"

"Lena is the *most* proud," she told him, sparing a second to give him the quickest of scratches behind his ear before picking up the other end of the collar.

If this worked, she'd be saving the city *and* forcing the giants to listen to what she had to say.

And if it didn't, well, at least Rufus could still get away.

"Be ready to use your boots, okay, little man?" she said to him, threading one end of the collar into the other.

His whiskers twitched. "We run now?"

"If things go badly, then yes, you *run*."

He started to protest, but she couldn't wait any longer: the giants had gotten too close, and in another minute or so, they'd step over the near side of the collar. It had to be now.

Lena whispered a silent prayer, then buckled the collar.

Instantly, everything encircled by the collar shrank down to one-tenth of its size. The buildings—the few that remained, at least—the trees, the grass, *everything* in that part of town suddenly was no bigger than a dollhouse.

And most importantly, the group of five giants—four guards and their king—were now very much human-sized, *Lena*-sized, and looking *very* surprised at that fact.

It had worked. Lena almost couldn't believe it. It'd *worked*!

The collar *should* keep everything shrunken down too, as long as the buckle was closed, even if they stepped outside of it. And since they didn't know what had happened to them, keeping it closed shouldn't be a problem.

And now she could save the city, and maybe even convince the giants they'd been wrong about humans altogether!

"Um, we eat people?" asked one of the now human-height giant guards, looking confused.

Okay, so maybe they'd need a minute to recover from the air sickness first.

"All of you, *stay calm*!" Lena shouted to them, leaving Rufus behind as she sprinted over to where the giants stood. "It's going to be okay!"

"What . . . what did you do to us?" said a second guard, sounding a bit more normal now that the thick air wasn't affecting him as much. He looked at the others. "Did we *really* say we were going to eat people?"

The guards all gave each other embarrassed glances, and Creel blushed. "I guess air sickness *is* real," he said. "Everything was so foggy!"

Lena stopped short just in front of them as the giants turned to face her, preparing for a fight. *"You!"* King Denir shouted, his face contorted with rage, even without the air sickness. "You did this to us! You defiled us by turning us human. Restore us this minute!"

"Well, maybe she can let us catch our breath first?" asked Creel, before giving his king an apologetic look.

"Do you see how *ridiculous* this all was?" Lena said to them, pointing at the destruction they'd left behind. "Look around you! These were people's homes, their lives! And you were destroying them because you thought they stole the Spark, which they *didn't*." She sighed. "*I* did, by accident, and you knew it was me, Your Majesty. Punish me if you want, but leave these poor people alone."

The king's face turned bright red. "You *dare* speak to me this way after everything you've done, you little human thief?"

Lena's insides twisted, and she almost looked away but forced herself to hold the king's gaze. "I am a *giant*," she said quietly. "I don't care if you believe it or not. And take a look at yourselves! Aren't *you* all giants still, no matter how large you are now?"

"You're *no* giant," the king said, ignoring her question as he strode toward her. "You're a thief and a liar, and that says *human* to me. No *true* giant would ever have a child of your size. And no true giant would ever speak to, let alone *befriend* one of these horrible humans."

"You . . . you don't get to say that to me," she whispered, looking away for just an instant. "Not about my parents, and not about *me*. It's not right. It's not *true*."

"Of course it's true," the king hissed, moving in closer. "I don't know if the giants who raised you found you somewhere, a little human baby left all alone, or if they took you on purpose. But you are *no* giant, and you *never* will be."

His words echoed in her mind, just like they had at the ritual.

You are no *giant. You are* no *giant. You are* no *giant.*

And oddly, Lena realized that as much as his words hurt . . . she was just so *tired* of hearing them. So tired of his hate, so tired of trying to convince the others, trying to prove her giant-hood, trying to change their narrow minds.

Like Jin had said, the other giants were the ones with a problem, the king most of all. And no cauldron or genie spell needed to tell her how she felt inside, and who she was.

"You keep saying I'm not a giant," she said quietly. "I don't think you know what that would mean, though."

The king sneered. "You think a human is smarter than a giant? Of course I know what that means. It means you're less than us, not worthy to walk the same land. You're a thief, like the rest of your kind."

Lena shook her head, strangely numb to his insults. *Huh,* she thought. "No. You're still missing the point, what a giant is, and what a giant does."

She watched as the words slowly worked their way into his head, and realization hit his eyes. He took a step backward, but it was already too late.

"Giants *fight* to show their *might,*" Lena continued,

narrowing her eyes. "Your words, Your Majesty. So if I *am* a giant, I guess it's time to prove it."

The king's nostrils flared with anger. "You *dare*—"

Lena punched him in the face, knocking him all the way back almost out of the city altogether.

"I sure do," she said, smiling widely.

CHAPTER 34

The Golden King leaned forward on his throne, squinting into the distance. "The giants have disappeared," he said, sounding surprised. "How is that possible? They barely destroyed half the city! Can we not count on them for *anything*?"

Jin shrugged. "Who can say?"

The king gave him a suspicious glance as the people below seemed to realize the same thing and started running back into the city, away from the Faceless army. "If the giants are gone, there's nothing to stop the Cursed City's rebel supporters from fleeing in that direction. I don't want to be here all day, running them down."

"Right?" the Invisible Cloud of Hate said. "We all just hate being inconvenienced when we're on a murderous rampage."

"Genie," the king continued, "I wish for you to teleport all of us to the back of the city . . . and make us invisible and silent. Let's see what happened to the giants before we make ourselves known."

Jin sighed, wishing he'd been able to get Lena to safety before the king had pulled him back. As it was, he could sense her next to some curiously tiny buildings, which probably meant that whatever had happened to the giants was because of her. So the last thing he wanted was for the king to get a closer look and maybe focus on Lena again.

But what choice did he have? He cast the relevant spells, sending the Faceless army and siege tower to the back of the city, now both unseen and unheard by anyone outside the magic.

"Are *those* the giants?" the king asked as they arrived, pointing down at four human-sized men, with a fifth lying on the ground in a daze.

Jin didn't answer, his own eyes locked on Lena, standing before the four men, looking ready to fight. He clenched his own fists, wondering how badly the king would punish him if he just sent her a few miles away.

The punishment wouldn't be pleasant, but moreover, it'd be useless: he'd just wish for you to bring her back.

I really hate when you're right, you know.

Oh, I know.

"She *hit* me!" the giant on the ground said, slowly pushing to his feet, only to fall back to the ground. "*Get* her!"

Three of the giants moved toward Lena, but stopped as someone shouted out from behind the girl. "Look!" the fast cookie man yelled, and Jin glanced over to find him leading half the city toward the giants, all the residents looking *extremely* angry. "Lena brought them down to *our* size. Get them!"

"Wait!" Lena shouted, waving her hands to get the crowd's attention as she moved between the mob and the giants. "There's no need to fight anymore. They're not dangerous now!"

"Not dangerous?" the annoying chicken yelled, holding a pile of eggs under one wing. "Those monsters destroyed my henhouse and could have squished us all!"

"Yeah, they said they were going to eat us!" shouted the man who lived in the pumpkin. "I say we eat *them*!"

"Yikes," said a voice from Jin's side, the Invisible Cloud of Hate. Apparently, he'd magicked her along with the rest of the siege tower . . . or she'd taken enough of an interest just to follow them. "I take back every horrible thing I ever said about this city, just so I can say it ten times as bad. These people will mob up for any little thing!"

"Okay, no one's eating anyone," the wooden puppet said, trying to regain some control. As the crowd began to boo, he changed his tactic quickly. "Because we have to show them what we do to people who'd wreck our town!"

The mob roared in agreement, then swarmed toward Lena.

"This is fun," the Golden King said as Jin watched anxiously, waiting for his moment to secretly teleport Lena away. "But I want the city destroyed. Genie, I wish for you to restore the giants to their normal size, but without revealing our presence just yet."

Jin sighed heavily. Couldn't he at least wish for *easy* things?

The cauldron Lena had earlier, the Cauldron of Truth, the cosmic knowledge said. *That would do it . . . sort of.*

Sort of?

Well, it would turn them into their truest form, so theoretically it would restore their regular height. It just might do more *than that.*

Close enough, Jin thought, then teleported the cauldron over from where he'd thrown it to a spot right next to the giants.

"That's Mrs. Hubbard's cauldron!" someone shouted. "Where did they get that?"

"What?" Lena said, turning in surprise. "Don't let them near it! They could use it to turn back—"

"That's . . . a Cauldron of Truth!" one of the giants shouted. "It must be one of the last remaining in the world!"

Jin took a deep breath to try to calm himself as the Golden King began to giggle creepily. "Perfect," the king said. "That's just the thing. I can't believe this town had a Cauldron of Truth just lying around. They really are their worst enemy."

Maybe not their worst *enemy,* Jin thought. *Considering you. But definitely a close second.*

"Bring it here!" the giant on the ground shouted, and the three giants near the cauldron picked it up and carried it back to him, even as the mob surged forward.

"Creel, don't let him use it!" Lena shouted at the one giant standing apart, the one who'd identified the cauldron. "You don't know what it might show!"

"Afraid of seeing what a *true* giant looks like, girl?" the giant on the ground shouted as the others dropped the cauldron in front of him, then helped him to his feet. "Once I'm back to my normal size, I'll crush this entire city myself!"

The crowd slowed to a halt at this, looking at each other nervously. "Who brought the cauldron here?" someone shouted.

"Whoever it was, get them!" someone else yelled, and everything descended into chaos.

"No!" Lena shouted, surging forward, but two of the giants grabbed her, holding her in place, as the giant king dipped his hands into the cauldron, then drank greedily from it.

He instantly began to grow, a wild look in his eyes as his size returned to normal. The giants holding Lena had to step back to avoid being crushed, dragging her along with them, as the one she'd called Creel watched nervously. The mob now realized there was a new danger and began pointing and screaming in terror, several of them fleeing back into the city.

"Whoa, now that's a *big* boy," the Invisible Cloud said, whistling softly. "Reminds me weirdly of a giant my father and I faced after it swallowed this guy I hated. Kinda bittersweet, taking the giant down, is what I'm saying."

The growing giant began laughing, matching the Golden King's own giggling. "Do you see, girl?" he shouted, looking into the sky as he grew. "*This* is a true giant! The power to crush you *all* is mine, and no one will ever take it from me again!"

And then he looked down at the assembled mob below, and his expression changed.

"What . . . no! They're everywhere!" he shouted, his face contorting with terror as he took a step back, shaking the ground beneath his feet.

"Your Majesty?" one of the giants holding Lena shouted up. "Are you okay?"

"No, you fool!" he shrieked, looking around at the Cursed City's residents in horror. "The humans, they're all around us. Run, before they kill you, too, like they did my brother!"

And with that, he turned away from the city and fled screaming, his long strides taking him right over the Faceless army.

The Golden King turned to watch him go, then shrugged. "Well, *that* was dramatic. Still, not entirely helpful. I suppose it's time for the Faceless to wrap things up." He nodded at Jin. "I wish for them to be visible once again. It's time for them to wipe this city *out*."

CHAPTER 35

Your Majesty!" the giant guards shouted, and turned to follow their king.

"No, wait!" Creel yelled, holding up a hand to stop them. "Don't you smell that? There's something out there!"

Lena, barely able to believe what the cauldron had just done to King Denir, looked at Creel in confusion. She sniffed the air, and her eyes widened.

Giants' sense of smell had always been a bit better than humans, and Creel was right, because right now she could smell the armor of the Faceless men.

But the giant guards either ignored him or didn't care as they ran after their king . . . only to come up short as an entire army faded into view in their way.

"The Faceless!" someone shouted from the mob, and they

began screaming again, running in multiple directions. But it was too late: the Faceless must have encircled them all while invisible, as the empty-helmeted knights were behind them as well.

"Form up in a circle!" Lena shouted, pulling out her compass arrow and waving it in the air to get people's attention. "Protect the most vulnerable, put them in the center!"

Lil immediately went clucking into the middle of the forming circle, joining the egg Humphrey and a few others, while Creel, Lena, and the toughest of the townspeople protected them, facing out in every direction as the Faceless advanced.

And then the Faceless attacked, and everything turned into chaos.

People cried out as they were struck by the Faceless's magic-absorbing swords, and many fell to the ground, writhing around as whatever curse they'd been struck by disappeared. Mr. Ralph's arm turned human again where he was struck, and he stared down at it in shock. One of the Frog Prince's entourage frogs was struck and exploded into an old man who looked at his now-human body and began to wail in sadness.

A few of the villagers were able to fight back, using an assortment of rusted pitchforks or rakes, but their makeshift weapons wouldn't last for long against the Faceless's swords. There were just too many of them and not enough Cursed City residents who could fight.

The giant guards made themselves useful at least, since their strength hadn't shrunk with their bodies. But without swords themselves, they'd soon be hit by the Faceless's weapons, and who knew what would happen next. Would the giants regain their size? Or would the swords take away whatever magic had made them giants in the first place? Lena wasn't looking forward to finding out, as having to face three airsick giant guards *and* the Faceless was not something she wanted to think about.

"Stay in the circle!" she shouted, swinging her compass arrow to hold the Faceless off the centaur doctor. One of their swords had cut him deep in his horse hindquarters, and the back of his horse half disappeared into his human torso, turning him fully human again. Another Faceless swung at her, and she managed to knock its sword into the air, but just barely, as her compass arrow kept trying to swing her in the direction of a large wooden tower that had appeared with the Faceless.

She looked in that direction and saw the Golden King and Jin watching from above. But even worse, she could just barely make out the Last Knight behind the king, chained up and captured.

At first, seeing him tied up made her feel even worse about their chances. But what if she could free him? The knight might be able to turn the tide of the battle all on his own. She'd trained with him enough times to know his speed was completely unnatural, too fast to even see.

But if she left the fight to rescue the Last Knight, she'd be abandoning the remaining residents. They could be overrun, even with Creel's and the other giants' help!

She growled in frustration, hating that she had to choose, while still knowing she had no choice.

"Rufus!" she shouted, and he came running over to her from the center of the circle where he'd hid, the bravest boy in the whole world, considering how scared she knew he was. She picked up the now completely human former-centaur doctor and tossed him over Rufus's back. "Get him to Treats Lady, he's hurt!"

"I do it, Lena!" Rufus shouted, then blurred out as he used his Seven League Boots to leap right through the battlefield. Now that she didn't have to worry about the centaur anymore, she leapt straight into the Faceless, knocking into the three nearest her with both her shoulder and her compass arrow, hoping to draw them away from the residents as she pushed toward the Golden King and the Last Knight.

Except something scratched her right arm, and then her left, and she felt them both go limp, a numbness traveling through them. One of the Faceless grabbed her arms, and she tried to pull herself free, only to find her giant strength completely gone.

Lena growled in anger, then switched tactics and dove forward, pulling the Faceless holding her arms with her by using her still-powerful leg muscles. She somersaulted, just like the knight had taught her, and sent the creature flying into another Faceless, then jumped back to her feet, readying her compass arrow.

But the sight she found before her made her pull up short, even in the middle of the battle. Because somehow, the two Faceless she'd just crashed together had lost parts of their armor, one its leg and the other its arm.

And hanging from both empty sockets were tiny *people*, attached to what looked like an elaborate set of pulleys and levers.

"**There's been a breach!**" said multiple miniature men in both sets of armor at almost the same time. The minute warriors unhooked themselves and began to disappear in miniscule bursts of magical light even as she tried to make sense of what was happening.

The Faceless were just a bunch of six-inch men in armor, working together? But . . . but . . . *what*?

Something slammed into her from behind, knocking her into the now-empty Faceless armor on the ground in front of her. She kicked back automatically and took down another Faceless, but this time she grabbed his helmet before he could stand back up and yanked it off, then peered down inside as best she could.

Several tiny faces looked up at her in alarm.

"What *are* you?" she said, reaching in to grab one. "And why are you attacking us?"

"**Retreat!**" the tiny man in her hand shouted, along with the others. The inside of the armor lit up in that same magical light, but Lena refused to let her captive go: she leaned down and grabbed a Faceless's sword from the ground, then touched the point to the creature's tiny hand.

He immediately yelped in pain . . . and stayed put, robbed of whatever magic had been about to teleport him away.

"Aha!" Lena shouted in triumph. "Now we're getting somewhere!"

Except the rest of the battle had gone badly while she'd been distracted. Most of the Cursed City residents were now either captives of the Faceless or had been injured by their swords, causing a variety of wild effects. A nutcracker guard had turned entirely to wood, while the former donkey with a great love for cabbages was now a human with donkey ears . . . still carrying cabbages.

This couldn't go on. They needed the Last Knight, if they were going to have a chance of saving anyone!

One of the giants roared out in pain as a Faceless sliced into his arm with its sword. That arm instantly grew back to giant size, crashing into several Faceless as it did, then reduced back down to human-sized again, which must have been the multiple magics in effect on the giant. That had been lucky, but the next hit might not be. They *needed* the knight!

She tied the tiny man from the Faceless armor up in some thread from her pouch, then tossed him into her infinite pouch for safekeeping as she turned back to the siege tower where the king waited . . . and Jin, as well.

For a genie who seemed to be on everyone's side at least once, he certainly got around. But he and the king could wait. The knight was the important thing.

She narrowed her eyes, then used the strength still in her legs to leap over to the siege tower. She landed just beside it, then balanced herself and kicked out, taking out the entire bottom of the wooden tower.

As it began to collapse, Lena quickly moved aside, hoping the knight wouldn't get hurt in the fall. Above, she heard the king yell, "I wish you to save us!"

She heard Jin mutter something angrily, but he and the king appeared next to Lena on the ground as the siege tower collapsed.

Except he hadn't brought the knight, who had tumbled into the rubble along with the rest of the tower. If the Last Knight ended up hurt, that could end the battle right there. . . .

"You!" the king shouted, pulling Lena's attention back to him and the genie. "This is the second piece of my property you've dared lay your hands on today. I am getting rather *annoyed*!"

"Well, *good*!" Lena shouted back, not knowing what else to do. "You're a terrible person, and annoyed is the least of what you deserve to feel!"

The Golden King sneered, then turned to Jin. "Listen carefully, genie, as there will be no loopholes in this one. I wish for you to *destroy* this girl, once and for all!"

CHAPTER 36

Jin felt his entire body go cold, and he turned to stare at the king in shock. "Your . . . Your Majesty, there's no need to—"

"I said *destroy her!*" the Golden King shouted. The king held up his clenched fist. "Do it *now* or I'll crush the very life from your worthless self!"

Before he could even respond, Jin's body folded in on itself, and agony spread like lightning through every inch. The pain was too intense to resist, and he knew he couldn't keep from fulfilling the king's wish.

But he also couldn't harm the one person he'd met who wasn't completely terrible! What kind of genie would he be if he went around destroying innocents?

THERE ARE *NO INNOCENTS!*

Weren't you the one who ruined a bunch of lives on your first wish? Just admit that you're selfish and like this girl.

The voices were *not* helping, either with his decision or the pain.

Jin looked up at Lena through the pain and watched as she quickly picked up one of the shadow-magic swords from an unconscious Faceless. She aimed it in his direction, probably hoping to stop whatever magic he used on her, but Jin knew she'd be far too late.

I'm sorry, he mouthed silently to her, not knowing what else to say. And weirdly, he found he really *was* sorry. For tricking her, for using her to find the Last Knight, and for causing all this horribleness in the first place.

"Do it!" the king roared, sending another wave of pain through Jin.

A scream emerged without Jin even consciously knowing he was doing it. He couldn't hold on. The king's control over him would never lessen, never allow him any sort of freedom. The ring gave control over Jin to a human, and there was nothing he could do about it.

Well, almost nothing. He did still have the Spark.

YES! the magic screamed in his head. *BREAK FREE*

FROM YOUR ELDERS' RULES AND CHOOSE YOUR OWN PATH. WE WILL SHOW THESE EARTHBOUND CREATURES WHO IS IN CONTROL, AND WHO IS DESTINED TO SERVE!

In spite of the pain, Jin slowly smiled. *That's not what I meant.* . . . *WHAT?*

I'm sorry, but you're a little too much like the king, Jin thought at the magic. *And I don't need another one of* those *in my life.*

There was a pause, and then a wave of anger came from the Spark. *WHAT ARE YOU DOING? DON'T ALLOW THEM TO CONTROL YOU! RELEASE MY POWER, AND LET IT WASH OVER THE WORLD SO THAT WE MIGHT RULE TOGETHER!*

Release your power? Jin almost laughed. *That's the plan!*

And with that, in spite of the magic's previous insistence that he couldn't, Jin expelled the Spark from his body.

The pain was almost worse than what the king was inflicting. Every inch of Jin felt like it was burning in an eternal flame, and he screamed with all his spirit, just hoping for it to end, but not believing it ever would.

And then the Spark was free, emerging like a ball of fire without its bowl to hold it. As the pain of its expulsion disappeared, Jin could feel the Spark's fury at him over his rejection of it, and he quickly froze it in midair before it latched onto anyone else.

He glanced up at Lena, who looked more surprised than anything. "Stab it!" he shouted at her. "If you don't, the king will find a way to use it!"

"What?" the Golden King shouted. "I ordered you to destroy her! You cannot disobey me!"

The pain doubled this time, something Jin wouldn't have believed possible. But even through the agony, he could see Lena step forward with the sword. She raised it, aiming carefully, and then drove it straight down . . .

Right at the Golden King's hand, the one with Jin's ring.

The sword struck true, and the king's hand fell to the ground, erasing all traces of Jin's agony as the king lost his ring. Jin looked up in shock, not able to believe what she'd just done.

Except the king didn't seem even the least bit hurt. Instead, he slowly grinned as black light pushed out of his wrist, and from the hand on the ground below him. The two lights met up, and the hand slowly rose back up toward the king.

"You have no *idea* what you're dealing with," the king said, his eyes turning black with shadow magic. "There's a darkness coming for this land, and it will destroy all light in its path!"

"What *is* he?" Lena asked, stepping back away from the king as Jin did the same.

"No idea," he said, shaking his head. "But we need to get rid of the Spark."

"Do not touch it!" the king shouted, reaching for the Spark with his golden glove. Lena flung her compass arrow out to knock his glove away, though, and this time the Golden King shouted in pain and annoyance. The arrow landed on the ground, solid gold now and pointing straight at Jin.

"Spark!" Lena shouted, shoving her hand directly into the fire and closing her eyes. "Return to your Sparktender!"

"NO!" the king shouted, but it was too late. The Spark disappeared in a burst of fire, presumably teleporting itself to whatever a Sparktender was, just as the king's hand merged back with his wrist.

Instantly, the pain returned, and Jin cried out, lights exploding before his eyes. "You shall *pay* for your betrayal!" the king shouted, aiming his golden glove toward Lena to keep her from interfering. "You deserve the same fate as the pathetic creatures in this city!"

"Well, that's just rude," said a new voice, and Jin froze, not believing it. He looked up at the king to find a small egg with arms and legs hanging from the man's hand, just about to remove the ring from his finger. "And honestly," Humphrey said, "as disappointed as I am in Mel, I think I can forgive him if he had *you* forcing him to do all of this."

"What . . . *no!*" the king shouted. Humphrey—no, Humpty, that was what his friends called him—Humpty the egg pulled Jin's ring off the Golden King's finger and tumbled to the ground with it. Of course Humpty cracked as he hit, but that didn't stop him, and he quickly took off, hobbling out of the king's reach.

"Humpty, you're a genius!" Jin shouted, standing back up straight as once again he found himself pain-free. "Just don't give that ring to *anyone.*"

"I won't give it to just anyone!" Humpty shouted. "I'll give it to the Last Knight!"

And with that, Jin's whole body went ice cold. "No, please!" he shouted, as the little, horrible egg disappeared into the knight's chains, and Jin could feel the ring's control take hold once more.

"Well, isn't *that* something," said the Last Knight, still chained up, but now with one hand sticking out of his binds, the ring on his finger. "Ah, genie? Any chance you have a wish left in you? Because I have a few ideas of what to do with the king here."

The Golden King looked between Lena, Jin, and the Last Knight, then sneered. "*Enough* of this. You haven't won anything. The shadow is more powerful than ever and will destroy this city soon enough. And you three will suffer unlike any others!"

Behind him, a circle of black void opened in the air, and two small children, a boy and a girl, stepped out of it, their eyes as black as the shadow behind them.

"You *cannot* have him," the little boy said, and reached out his hand.

"He is the shadow's," said the little girl, and did the same.

Black light passed from their hands to surround the king, and he began to laugh as the shadow covered his eyes as well.

"No!" the Last Knight shouted. "Grab those twins, someone! *They're* the ones controlling the shadow magic!"

But before anyone could move, the black light pulled the Golden King and the two identical children back inside the circle, which disappeared in a burst of shadow magic, along with the Faceless army.

Jin just stared in surprise, not at all sure what to say.

Unfortunately, not everyone was as speechless as he was.

"Yay!" Humpty shouted from a few yards away. "I saved everyone. I'm a *hero*!" He glanced over at Jin. "But would you mind taking me back to the horse doctor? I'm feeling a bit cracked over here."

CHAPTER 37

That's really your first wish?" Jin shouted, loud enough that Lena covered her ears. "You can't be serious."

The Last Knight laughed. "It's more of a request. I'd give up the ring, but then someone dangerous might find it, like the Golden King did, so why don't you stay here for a while until we figure out how to permanently free you?"

The genie growled something Lena couldn't hear. "I already *know* . . . oh, forget it. If your wish is really for me to help rebuild the city, then *fine*, I'll do it. But this *does* count as a wish, and no wishing for more wishes!"

"I'd *never*," the knight said indignantly, putting his hand over his heart as Jin slowly floated away, throwing a look back at Lena as he did, then blushing and turning away again to get started on the cleanup.

"Well," Lena said with a sigh. "This all went much worse than I could possibly have imagined."

"Oh, it's not a win by any stretch," the knight said. "But I think it could have been worse. And look, we have a new friend. He's much nicer than the last genie I knew, though that could be because that genie was stuck in a mirror, answering the Wicked Queen's questions for years."

"He's a better person, or genie, than I gave him credit for," Lena said, watching Jin go with a smile. "He really went through a lot to keep from destroying me. And he gave me some advice a little earlier that honestly helped a lot."

"Huh," the knight said, nodding. "Maybe he *does* have potential. Let's see how he gets along with the city's residents."

"You want *another* pumpkin?" Jin shouted at Peter from a dozen yards away. "Oh, so what, you think I can just magic you up one? Why don't you climb a beanstalk and steal some seeds from a giant like a normal person?"

"Whoa, no stealing from giants!" Lena shouted, and Jin waved at her in a friendly way, then turned back to whisper something to Peter, pointing up into the clouds.

"Okay, so maybe 'potential' is a strong word for . . . whatever it is he has," the knight said, and Lena laughed slightly.

"Couldn't you just free him?" she asked. "You know, wish for him to no longer be controlled by anyone?"

"Apparently not," the knight said with a shrug. "He mumbled something about how *that* loophole of all things was closed. But even then, I'm not sure I really want to unleash someone with his kind of power on the unsuspecting world just yet."

Lena frowned, not sure she agreed, but if it wouldn't work anyway, there wasn't much to be done.

They both silently watched Jin for a moment, before the knight turned to her. "What about you?"

"What *about* me?" Lena said. "Are you asking if *I* should be unleashed on an unsuspecting world?"

The knight laughed again. "In a way. I meant, what are you going to do?"

Lena winced, feeling her insides tighten up at the question. "I can't go home. Whatever the king is now, he's not going to just let me come back like nothing happened."

"You could stay here," the knight said. "Mrs. Hubbard would love to have you, and truthfully, I could use more help against the Golden King. Our rebellion is basically down to just me, and maybe Jin, if I use up another wish on it."

She bit her lip, considering this. "What was that all about, with those kids? The small children?"

The knight turned to her like he was going to explain, then shook his head. "Don't worry about it for now. Just some . . . family issues, and it's my problem to fix. If you stay, I'll leave you to deal with the Faceless. You seem to have a talent for it." He waved his hand at the destroyed town, where the Faceless had attacked.

Lena didn't answer right away, watching as Jin and Peter pulled a third resident into their conversation, all three pointing up at the sky now. The Cursed City had always felt like a second home, especially with Mrs. Hubbard and her other friends. And the residents already seemed to feel guilty about how they'd treated her, throwing her apologetic looks as they passed.

The knight's offer made sense, and she knew she should take it. But just one thing had to come first.

"I'm in," she said, turning back to him. "But before we get started, I have to say a proper goodbye to my parents."

The knight tilted his head. "I thought you said you couldn't go home."

She grinned and patted Rufus's head as he purred softly beside her. One of the city's fairies was floating closer to the cat, a hand outstretched to pet him as her friends urged her on. But Rufus let out an overly loud sigh, and all three fairies went flying.

"Oh, I think we can find a way to sneak in for a quick visit." Lena paused, then remembered something. "By the way, I almost forgot this in all the fighting. I found out what the Faceless are."

The knight froze in surprise. "You *what*?"

Lena reached into her pouch and pulled out the still-bound tiny person she'd kept from teleporting away. The brown-haired creature glared angrily at her, and she started to hand him over to the knight, then paused.

She'd assumed the creature had been an adult when she'd captured him, but now that she had a chance to really examine him, he was clearly just a boy. And weirdly, she could have sworn she'd seen him somewhere before. His hair looked familiar, if nothing else.

She shook her head, then gave him to the knight.

"Do you . . . recognize him? I mean, considering that you . . ." She trailed off, not wanting to speak the knight's secret out loud.

He shook his head. "No, but I'll interrogate him and find

out what he knows." He tucked the tiny boy into his own pouch, then looked back up at her. "You did good work, Lena. Now go say goodbye to your parents."

Lena grinned. "I just have one quick stop before that."

The remaining giant guards had surrounded Creel, the Sparktender, and were throwing dirty looks at anyone who got close. A few of the Cursed City residents looked like they still might want to pick a fight, but the guards' strength clearly intimidated them.

"Lena," Creel said as she approached, Rufus at her side. "I'm so sorry about how this all went. I probably should never have invited you to the ritual in the first place."

She forced a smile as the guards slowly separated, giving them a bit of room. "I'm . . . glad you did, if only so I could see it for once. I'm so sorry for taking the Spark, Creel. I never intended to, but I just didn't know what it could do."

"Honestly, neither did I," he admitted, looking down at the Spark. He'd found a shattered piece of pottery somewhere, and now the flame was floating in it. "So it seems as if I have some researching to do."

"Maybe I'll check around down here," Lena said with a shrug. "I'll try to get you a message if I find anything."

Creel nodded, then looked up at Lena. "Thank you for returning it intact." He paused, looking at the guards, then moved in closer. "And before we go . . ."

Lena gasped as Creel took her hand and gently placed it into the flame.

"Lena, daughter of Roral the Unburdened and Cedra the Terrifying," he chanted as Lena's eyes widened. "I now declare you on your path toward adulthood and give you a true name. From now on, you will be known as Lena the *Giant*, and all shall so recognize you."

Jin had a few different plans going by the time he decided he'd done enough for his first day of repairing the Cursed City and went to look for the Last Knight to let him know. Granted, his first day had lasted all of maybe a half hour, but there was no use jumping into things too quickly.

According to Peter, the Last Knight had been asked to stay in the city for now, at least until Mrs. Hubbard could get the misdirection spell back up, since there was no way of knowing if the Golden King would try attacking again. No one thought it would happen right away, but it was only a matter of time.

Jin followed various people's directions until he found the knight's new residence, apparently the home of the nutcracker who'd been turned entirely to wood. It was just a temporary thing until the nutcracker could be restored with the rest of the town, so Mrs. Hubbard clearly had her work cut out for her.

Jin floated up to the door and started to knock, only to hear voices on the other side, including one he'd never heard before. Wondering what was going on, he turned himself invisible and insubstantial, then pushed himself through the door just enough to see inside.

Whatever he would have guessed, the truth was something far, far weirder.

Climbing out of the Cauldron of Truth was a tiny, human-looking boy. "Thank you, Sir Thomas," the boy said, shaking his head. "That feels *so* much better. So you've used this on others of us enchanted by the shadow magic?"

"Dozens by now," said the knight, only his voice was clearer than Jin had ever heard before. He glanced in the direction of the man's armor, and his eyes widened.

A second tiny person stood where the Last Knight's helmet usually was. Inside, an elaborate pulley-and-lever system seemed to allow the man to operate the armor from the helmet.

"Tell our people," this Thomas said from within the knight's armor, "that I *will* return and free them. The shadow magic rules them now, but I will soon have a way to take its power for my *own*. All I need are the twins, and it will be mine to control as it was once the Wicked Queen's. And then I will use it against the true oppressors of this world!"

"What about the twins?" the boy asked.

"I forced the Golden King to send them into the shadowlands, thinking it was for their protection," the small knight said. "All it took was him thinking I'd break into his castle and steal them back. He's always been easy to manipulate when it comes to his treasures."

"So they'll be within reach," the boy said, nodding. "I'll tell the others, then. Good luck, Sir Thomas."

"To you as well, Shefin," Thomas said.

The boy paused, then looked up at the Last Knight. "That girl who found me. She seemed . . . fascinating, somehow. There was something about her—"

Jin's eyes narrowed, and he glared at this newcomer.

But Thomas just smiled. "Don't worry. You'll be seeing her again. She's one of us, don't you doubt it. Now get home, spread the word of what's to come."

The boy nodded, then saluted the knight and disappeared in a burst of light.

The tiny knight sighed, then glanced up in Jin's direction, just as Jin instinctually yanked his head back out of the door, not that it would have mattered, considering he was invisible. For a moment, he couldn't help but float in place, trying to figure out exactly what it was he'd just witnessed.

"See anything interesting?" said the Invisible Cloud of Hate from right next to him, making him jump almost out of his skin.

"I . . . what?" Jin whispered, having no idea what was happening.

"That about covers it," the Invisible Cloud of Hate said. "I'm just glad I'm not the only one who knows what the knight is up to. This whole time, he's pretended to be focusing on the Golden King, and all he really cares about is getting the king's shadow magic."

"But . . . why?" Jin asked.

"What am I, a Story Book? Go find that out yourself!" the cloud shouted. "I've been stuck here for months now, all because Captain Thomas there stole my sword."

"*Your* sword?" Jin said, feeling even more lost. "The glass one?"

"It's not glass, it's the sword of an Eye," the cloud said, and Jin could see her shape fading into view through his magical sense. "The Eyes were the Wicked Queen's spies, and Thomas there was our captain. Some of us called him Tom Thumb behind his back, because size jokes always annoyed him."

"And you were an Eye too, for this queen?" Jin said. "Did she call *herself* the Wicked Queen? Because that seems odd. Not many wicked people see themselves that way."

"That's your question?" the woman said.

"*Yes*, but it can wait," Jin said. "That's just . . . a lot of information. Why haven't you told the other people about this, if the knight is so bad?"

"I *tried*," the Invisible Cloud of Hate hissed. "But almost no one can see or hear me. Only those in touch with magic can even sense me, let alone communicate, which at the moment means . . . you."

"And who *are* you?" Jin asked, his mind reeling from all of this. He'd need to tell Lena, as she clearly idolized the knight.

He felt someone shake his invisible, insubstantial hand. "My name's Jillian," the Invisible Cloud of Hate said. "But my friends call me Jill, and since you're going to help me take the Last Knight down, we're going to be *good* friends."

"Jill?" Jin said, raising an eyebrow. "Never heard of you."

She snorted. "That's because the boys in my family get all the fame. It's always 'Jack' this or 'Jack' that. But now my brother and his wife are both golden statues, and their twins are running wild with shadow magic, so who's the good kid *now*, huh?" She paused. "Oh, we're going to need to free them, too, by the way. I'm so glad someone can finally *hear* me!"

Jin blinked, then blinked again. "I'm sorry . . . *what* now?"

Did you really not read that Half Upon a Time *Story Book I told you about when you first appeared?* the cosmic knowledge asked. *No wonder you've been so confused!*

You say a lot of useless things. How am I supposed to know which ones will later be important? Jin shouted back in his mind, then sighed deeply and turned back to the invisible Jill. "Okay. Back up. Start from the beginning. Who's this Jack guy, anyway?"

ACKNOWLEDGMENTS

Whoa, if only there were Story Books available for us to read about Jack's adventures! What a world that would be—wait a second . . . there ARE! How lucky can we even be?!

(Basically, this would be a great time to read the original Half Upon a Time series if you'd like some background on what Jill was just talking about. If not, though, don't worry, as you'll get everything you need to know in the next book!)

For all those readers who enjoyed the first series and are back for more, I want to thank you for putting your faith in me for three more books. You shouldn't have, though. Just wait till you see what happened to Jack, May, and everyone. *sad trombone*

And to all my new readers, welcome! I apologize for trying my best to make you cry.

All those tears aren't just my fault, though. The following

people are instrumental in causing all the feels you might feel throughout this series:

First, I have to thank my agent, Michael Bourret, and my two editors at Aladdin, Kara Sargent and Anna Parsons, for agreeing to all this madness, and shaping it into the book you have in your hands today. I also want to thank Valerie Garfield, my publisher at Aladdin; Nadia Almahdi in marketing; Cassie Malmo and Nicole Russo in publicity; Laura DiSiena, the designer of the book; production editors Elizabeth Mims and Olivia Ritchie; Michelle Leo and the education/library team; Stephanie Voros and the subrights group; Christina Pecorale and the whole sales team; and so much love to Vivienne To, the greatest cover artist ever, and pretty much solely responsible for anyone picking these books up.

See you in Book 2, and again, I'm so, so sorry about what's to come!

**THE ADVENTURE CONTINUES IN
TALL TALES. TURN THE PAGE
FOR A SNEAK PEEK!**

Once upon a time, Lena the Giant would never have imagined having an audience of her own kind as she fought her way through a patrol of Faceless, the Golden King's mind-controlled army. But everything was different now, after she'd received her epithet from the Sparktender, and the other giants had seen her for who she really was: a five-and-a-half-foot tall giant, just like the rest of them in every way but height.

"Rip 'em up!" her father shouted, his voice a bit muffled by a bubble of thinner air, to keep him from getting air sickness down on the ground. "That's my girl!"

The visit had started as a test of the new magical bubbles, only to be interrupted by a Faceless patrol. Fortunately, her guests had been more than happy to wait as Lena took out the

Golden King's soldiers. Her father in particular had offered to help, but Lena had refused, not wanting to share.

A Faceless in a full suit of black armor swung its magical sword at Lena, and she ducked beneath it, then kicked out, knocking the Faceless into a tree. It slid down the trunk, then lit up with small bursts of light as the brainwashed Lilliputians inside all teleported away.

"Aw, they're escaping!" Creel the Sparktender shouted.

Lena frowned, then pointed at the pile of Faceless armor she'd already accumulated. "I know, they're quick. But that's why I grab trophies whenever I can!"

"Just watch out for those swords of theirs!" her mother said, wincing as another Faceless drove his sword down, slamming it into the ground just inches from where Lena had been standing. "They'll take away your strength again!"

Her mother had a point: the last time Lena had actually been struck by one of their swords, she'd lost all of the giant power in her arms. Sure, it'd come back over the last few weeks, and she was finally feeling normal again, but that wasn't something she wanted to repeat.

At least for her, it'd just been strength. Half of the residents of the Cursed City had been hit as well, changing them back to their non-cursed forms, which almost none of them preferred. Just like her own power, though, the residents' magical curses had returned, and the entire city's population was back to normal. Or the Cursed City version of normal.

Except now the residents also knew Lena's secret, that she was actually just a very short giant, not the regular human they'd taken her for. At first they'd treated her with fear and paranoia, but after she'd helped save the city from the Golden King's army, they'd come around quickly.

"Behind you!" her father roared, almost knocking a few of the remaining Faceless off their feet with the power of his voice. Lena kicked back without looking and sent another Faceless flying into the woods.

"Lena," said Rufus, her horse-sized cat, as he trotted away from her mother's foot and settled himself down on the ground right in the middle of the battle, no longer afraid of the Faceless after fighting them with Lena so many times. "I am hungry. Treats?"

"Just a minute, little man," she said, punching another Faceless in the helmet, which went flying off. Without the protection of the headpiece, various tiny men and women inside quickly scrambled down farther into the armor, at which point several more bursts of light appeared as they teleported to safety.

These were Lilliputians, as small as giants were big, and the Last Knight's own people. For years they'd been infected by the Golden King's shadow magic, being forced to fight under his command. Fortunately, the Last Knight had used a magical item called the Cauldron of Truth on some captured Faceless to free their minds, and those Lilliputians had then returned to their homeland to help start a rebellion against the Golden King.

But there were far more Lilliputians still under the shadow's power than had been freed, and the king wouldn't let up until he destroyed the Cursed City. Unfortunately, without the Cauldron of Truth, all Lena could do was make sure these Faceless never got anywhere close. The city's protective spell had just about been restored, ensuring that no one with any bad intentions could even find the city. Mrs. Hubbard had spent countless hours the last few weeks working to get it back up, but the magic took time, and the city needed protecting.

And that's where Lena came in. After all, giants fight to show their might, as the saying went, and there was nothing Lena enjoyed more than getting to use her full strength to protect her friends and loved ones.

"Last one!" Creel shouted as a Faceless turned away from

Lena to stalk Rufus. She gasped, the idea that her cat might be in danger sending her into a fury, and leapt forward with all her strength. Her giant power propelled her straight into the Faceless, and she slammed the armor's torso right off its legs.

"Get 'em!" her father shouted as brainwashed Lilliputians came pouring out of the armor, each one equipped with their own magical teleportation device. Lena knew that if she could just grab one, she could bring them to the Last Knight and free the Lilliputian's mind.

But even with Rufus joining in to hunt the tiny people, it was quickly apparent that they were both too slow, as the Lilliputians all disappeared, leaving behind that same burst of magical light. Lena growled in frustration, but she really couldn't complain. After all, the Cursed City was safe, another Faceless patrol had been wiped out, and she'd even gotten to show off a bit for her parents and Creel.

"Look at you go, Lena!" her father shouted, pulling out a nearby tree and shaking it in excitement. Her mother and Creel both began clapping, and all three giants grinned widely. The praise hit Lena almost like a giant punch, and she took a step back in surprise. This was just all so new and *wonderful*, not having to hide her true size from other giants, and even getting to flaunt her strength for them. It was like nothing she was used to, and she never wanted it to end.

But even the giants' magical air bubbles wouldn't last forever, and she didn't want her family or Creel to suffer from air sickness, which fogged up giants' brains to the point they lost all control, and might potentially put the Cursed City in danger. So while she could have listened to their applause for another few days, it was time for them to climb back up the mountain to the giant village in the clouds.

"I'm so glad you could all come down to visit!" she shouted up at them. Her mother pushed one of her fingers into the ground, and Lena threw her arms around the finger, hugging it tightly. "Promise you'll come back soon!"

"We certainly will, now that we can do it safely!" Creel said, tapping the air bubble around his head. "And please thank that witch who came up with these again. They're just fantastic."

"I will!" Lena promised, knowing she owed Mrs. Hubbard big-time, and not just for the bubbles. The owner of the Boot-ique, a Cursed City store built within a discarded giant boot, Mrs. Hubbard had openly welcomed Lena when she'd first visited. There was no one in town that Lena owed more to, and that debt just kept growing. "But you should all go back now before the thinner air starts running out in there."

"Love you, Lena girl," her father said, his voice a bit gravelly as he sniffed. He tried to wipe a tear away, only to smack his finger against the air bubble, so he looked away instead. "We're just so proud. So, so proud."

Lena had to look away herself, though she couldn't hide her own loud sniff. She rubbed the back of her hand against her now-wet eyes, then waved at her parents and Creel as they turned to clomp back toward the mountain that once Lena had descended to explore the human world below the clouds.

"Treats *now*?" Rufus said, bumping his head into her impatiently. At his size, he almost knocked her over with every headbutt.

"Let me just tie up all the armor, okay?" she said, moving to do just that. "If we leave it out in the open, another patrol might find it, and figure out they're close to the city."

Rufus's ears flattened in irritation, but he helped collect various pieces of armor using his teeth as Lena snaked a rope through it all. A few moments later, she stood back up with a satisfied sigh and surveyed the field of battle.

"Not too bad," she said, nodding. "Didn't even knock down a tree this time. Other than that one Dad pulled up."

"Lena is the best," Rufus said through a mouthful of helmet. "Treats? Treats. Treats?"

She scratched behind his ears, then moved to grab the roped-together armor, happier than she'd ever been in her life. And the best part was, even with the threat of the Golden King out there, she knew that between herself, the Last Knight, and her genie friend Jin, they could handle it and keep everyone safe.

After all, with a genie on *their* side, what could possibly go wrong?

Join Jack and May on their
mixed-up fairy tale adventure in the
HALF UPON A TIME trilogy!

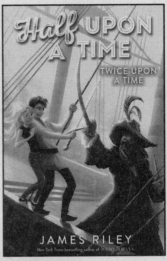

THE REVENGE OF MAGIC

Magic reawakens in this thrilling series from the
New York Times bestselling author of *Story Thieves*!

READ& LEARN
with
simon kids

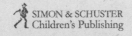